MAYA RUNNING

ALSO AVAILABLE FROM
LAUREL-LEAF BOOKS

MAYA RUNNING

ANJALI BANERJEE

Published by Laurel-Leaf
an imprint of Random House Children's Books
a division of Random House, Inc.
New York

Originally published in hardcover in the United States
by Wendy Lamb Books, New York, in 2005. This edition
published by arrangement with Wendy Lamb Books.

Laurel-Leaf and colophon are registered trademarks of
Random House, Inc.

www.randomhouse.com/teens

Educators and librarians, for a variety of teaching tools, visit us at
www.randomhouse.com/teachers

RL: 4.7
ISBN-13: 978-0-553-49424-2
ISBN-10: 0-553-49424-4
August 2006
Printed in the United States of America
10 9 8 7 6 5 4 3 2 1

FOR MY FAMILY

ACKNOWLEDGMENTS

Heartfelt thanks to my terrific agent, Winifred Golden; my editor, Wendy Lamb; and assistant editor Alison Meyer. Thanks also to my critiquers: Dotty, Janine, Kate, Lois, Pj, Rose Marie, Sandi, Sheila, Skip, Susan P., Susan W., Julie Weston and Byron Sacre's Thursday gang. My gratitude to Hedgebrook, an idyllic writing residency for women, for giving me Waterfall Cottage for a week. A special thank-you to my childhood friend, Richard Penner, the man with the photographic memory. Thanks also to Marian Blue and editors who've published my work—Janet McEwan, Pam McCully, Jack Smith, Elizabeth Lex and others.

My love and appreciation to my parents, Sanjoy Banerjee and Denise Kiser, for their helpful comments; and to my husband, Joseph Machcinski.

Thanks to Randy Kiser; Daniela Banerjee; my sisters, Nita, Nicole and Giuliana; my brother, Matteo; and Vicki and Joe Machcinski (Sr.). I value your support. Auntie Georgie, your stories of India continue to inspire me.

I consulted Uma Krishnaswami's informative and well-written book, *The Broken Tusk: Stories of the Hindu God Ganesha*, for Auntie's tales about Ganesh.

Be careful what you set your heart upon—for it will surely be yours.

—James Baldwin

MAYA RUNNING

ON DISPLAY

DAD drives while picking his nose, an eccentric habit of geniuses. I hunker down in the backseat, pull up my parka hood and go incognito. I am Invisible Future-Girl sent back in time to study embarrassing fathers.

In the passenger seat Mum pretends not to notice, irritation scrunched in her shoulders. She's decked out for reentry into the Indian world: woolen coat over turquoise sari, kohl rimming her eyes and a round, red bindi on her forehead.

Dad thinks he looks cool in corduroy jacket and

Clarks Wallabees. We're both wearing jeans. I don't want to be ethnic. I want to run on the tundra beneath the northern lights, make igloos or snow angels, write to Anne Frank in my diary or clean my closet and find a door into Narnia. I want to see John Travolta, my dreamboat, in that new movie *Grease*. I want to ride elephants through the Bengal jungle, the way my great-grandfather rode before he choked on a wishbone and died. I would rather be anywhere but here, going to the Gross house for supper.

"Why can't I stay home and study?" I ask. "Tomorrow is a school day, and I get bored at the Grosses."

"Ghose, not Gross," Mum says.

"Their boys are babies. I'm old enough to babysit myself."

"You are going, and that is final."

"Why don't you want to go, Maya-baby?" Dad says with a bruise in his voice. "They're my very oldest friends."

I roll my eyes. Everyone is Dad's Very Oldest Friend from the dawn of history when he lived in Darjeeling. If they speak in Bengali, I just nod and pretend to understand.

Mum and Dad shift into Conversation for Grownups. They discuss riots in communist West Bengal, the weather in British Columbia and political unrest in Quebec, where the Parti Québécois has made French the official provincial language and forbidden the use of

English on signs. By 1979, Dad says, Quebec might separate from Canada.

I'm glad to be living in Manitoba, where signs are in English and I can find my way around.

Dad stops picking, switches on the radio and whistles off-key to "Daydream Believer."

The Navigator Look comes into Mum's eyes. She keeps a permanent Manitoba map in her head. She points to the left. "Turn here and we'll be there in no time flat."

Dad swings past rows of spruce trees and telephone poles and snowy fields rolling away in the headlights.

The Ghose family lives in a stucco split-level on the outskirts of town. Inside, the house smells of sweaty armpit, not of home, and I go rigid when Mrs. Ghose, a wide woman in an orange sari, hugs me and pinches my cheeks. I drown in the folds of her belly.

She steps back and grabs my chin. "What is this in your mouth? Look, you have braces."

Heat pricks my cheeks. I close my lips over the metal. At first, the braces gashed my lips bloody; then the cuts healed. Now it is easy to forget the wires in my mouth until someone yells, "Look! You have braces!"

I do? When did that happen? Let me run to the mirror and see. As if elves climbed in and went to work while I slept.

Mrs. Ghose has already let go of my chin. She grabs our coats and pats Mum's cheek as if she's a little girl. I hear whistling in another room and the ping, pop, ping of an electronic game.

Mum and Dad head off to the right while Mrs. Ghose shoves me left, launches me like a missile into the family room, the dungeon where the two young Ghose boys are playing Pong, the tennis video game on TV, in color. They both have on polyester shirts under knit vests, cat's-eye glasses and high-water pants showing hairy calves and striped tube socks. Their extreme nerdiness doesn't seem to bother them.

"Snacks for you children?" Mrs. Ghose shouts. "Sahadev? Vishnu, for you? Drinks?"

"Yes, Ma! Fanta root beer." Vishnu is maybe seven years old, with rumpled hair, and underwear sticking out of his pants. He hardly resembles a great god who is everywhere, which is what his name means. Sahadev shakes his head vigorously, unable to tear his gaze from the bouncing white ball on TV. He's about nine.

"For you, choto-Maya?"

"No, thank you, Mrs. Ghose," I say politely. I am not *choto*, small, yet I have been sentenced to languish in the children's prison, and now I have to pee.

"Auntie Mitil! Call me Auntie!" Mrs. Ghose screams as she bustles away.

"Auntie Mitil," I say to myself. Mrs. Ghose doesn't feel like an aunt.

I wait for the right moment to ask where the washroom is, but the boys don't acknowledge me. They're at that age, I suppose, when all girls have cooties.

Thin strains of an evening raga stray in from the living room. The sitar twang zigzags on and on with no discernible tune. Dad loves sitar music, and often closes his eyes while he listens and hums along, tapping his fingers on his knee.

I imagine him laughing with the grown-ups in the living room, which might as well be on another planet. The smells of frying pakoras and curry swirl down through the atmosphere.

Sitting on the couch, I cross my arms and legs. A vacant spot inside me grows bigger the more the boys play and the grown-ups laugh. FOR RENT, FOR LEASE, ROOM INSIDE MAYA, the sign reads. The empty place is also endurance, a poised kind of waiting. Only I'm not sure yet what I'm waiting for.

"Boys, samosas! Maya! Come, come." Dr. Ghose bursts in then, a slight man with graying hair combed sideways over his balding head. He's a doctor, not the same kind of doctor that Dad is, not a nuclear engineer. I'm often forced to explain the difference. Dad studies two-phase flow, while Dr. Ghose studies intestinal flow. He's a GI man. I think of those little G.I. Joe dolls. The guns and uniforms and army helmets and boots are all molded from the same piece of plastic.

Dr. Ghose's mouth blows Bengali bubble-words, which the boys understand. I can tell by the way their bodies shift, the way they nod at the right moments. Bengali is part of their lives, like combing oil through their glistening hair or praying to Hindu gods.

Envy digs into me, a craving to understand Bengali.

"Baba, I'm not hungry," Sahadev whines, pushing the glasses up on his nose.

"Me either, I want to play," says Vishnu, the great god with his underwear showing.

"Ah, come, you love samosas, homemade, lovely, lovely," Dad says from the doorway. He does the Indian sideways head nod around Indian friends. It's like Halloween. He wears his Canadian costume for Canadians, the Indian costume for Indians.

As Indian tradition dictates, the children eat first. Mrs. Ghose and Mum hover in the background, filling plates and glasses. I sit very still and eat with knife and fork, keeping my elbows off the table, while the boys stuff their faces with their hands, smearing dahl around their mouths.

The adults' voices fade into a murmur of blood rushing in my ears.

"Look at Mayasri," Mrs. Ghose says. "She is being so good. Why can't you boys be so good? She is an example for you. Maya, have more rice and dahl? So thin you are. You are not eating. Kamala, has she become thin?"

This is what Indians say even if you weigh a thousand pounds. I am Skinny Future-Girl with buckteeth and braces.

"She keeps quite busy," Mum says. "Ballet, skating, cross-country skiing—"

"All those extracurricular activities? And her studies? She is doing well?"

6

"Quite well. Highly commended."

I am on display.

"Boys, Mayasri excels in her studies, dances the ballet and what are you doing? Playing video games. Lazy boys." Mrs. Ghose whacks Vishnu on the head hard enough to knock a chunk of samosa from his mouth. He grabs a spoon to fish a pakora from his glass of milk.

"She also plays the piano quite well," Mum says.

Mrs. Ghose's eyes nearly pop out of her head. "She will give the boys lessons?"

I want to say *No, thank you, I won't give your irritating great god any stupid piano lessons.*

"If she has time." Mum frowns, allowing me this much. Next to Mrs. Ghose, Mum looks young and slim and beautiful. She doesn't seem comfortable either. I bet she wants to run home and tear off the sari. But she's Indian. She grew up in Calcutta. She can speak the language, make Bengali food, and wear a bindi on her forehead. She can fit in if she wants to.

My throat closes over a lump of dry rice. A terrible idea occurs to me. This supper is a setup. Mrs. Ghose wants me to marry either Sahadev or Vishnu in one of those arranged marriages. Why else would I be here? I'll have to run away.

Now all the grown-ups crowd into the humid kitchen. I'm trapped in a Bengali movie without subtitles. As they talk, everyone laughs and cries at the right parts, while I sit clueless in the middle.

"Maya?"

"Yes?" I look up and blink. I have accidentally disappeared inside myself again. Mrs. Ghose—Auntie Mitil—stands across the table, staring.

I glance down, thinking maybe I dropped curry on my T-shirt. Everyone stares. Conversation dribbles down a drain. I wait for the marriage plan.

Mum has gone into the other room with Dad and Dr. Ghose. They're discussing a brass table imported from India.

Mrs. Ghose repeats the phrase in Bengali. A question.

My throat goes dry. I nod. Maybe a yes will suffice, or a shake of my head, but still she stares.

Sahadev throws a pakora at Vishnu's head, and the great god sticks out his tongue, letting a slop of chewed glop fall on his plate. Sahadev says *Ew* and snorts milk out his nose. The boys break into gales of laughter while Mrs. Ghose smiles with affection, her expression saying *You boys will fetch a huge dowry someday.*

That's the way things are in India. The girl moves into the boy's house and dumps loads of money on his family. This is one reason I think Dad wishes I was born a boy, his first and only child. What he doesn't know is I will never get married, so he won't have to worry about going broke.

This time Mrs. Ghose hurls the question, a spear with a poison tip.

Sickness comes to my stomach. I gulp. "I—don't—speak—Bengali."

Sahadev stops his spoon in midair. Vishnu closes his mouth. Mrs. Ghose's eyebrows fuse, pulling her face toward its center.

"*Bangla bola na!*" Slowly she shakes her head. Pity drips from her voice. "Ah, Maya."

"She doesn't speak Bengali?" Sahadev gazes up at his mother in disbelief.

"She doesn't, stupid," Vishnu hisses across the table.

"Why?" Sahadev stares at me.

I say nothing. My parents like to have their own secret language. In the other room, they shift easily back and forth between Bengali and English.

"What was your question?" My voice comes out way too Canadian. My words slide and bump into each other.

I don't belong here. I imagine saying *Excuse me, it's rude to speak in front of me as if I'm not even here, and we're not in India anymore, we're in Canada now.* I imagine getting up, walking out into the snow, hitching a ride home.

But I sit stupidly in my chair.

"*Bangla bola na!*" Mrs. Ghose's voice fills with wonder, as if I'm a rare shooting star. She turns and throws papadum to sizzle on the stove.

The matter is closed.

Sahadev and Vishnu return to their play fighting. I sit stunned, my mind whirling.

"Can I use your washroom?" I ask, nearly choking. Nobody replies. I say louder to Sahadev, who sits closest, "Washroom!"

He points to the door. "Upstairs."

I dash for solitude across the green shag carpet and up the stairs. Voices and sitar music drift from the lower level. For a short time, nobody will miss me. I stop to catch my breath and notice old yellowed photographs on the hallway walls. The Ghose ancestors gaze from their finery, flowing silk saris and heaps of jewelry. They sit in ornate chairs in palatial rooms. Wealth trickles from their shoes. How could these Ghoses have come from those Ghoses?

I wonder about my ancestors. Who were they? My great-grandfather was conservator of forests for Bengal, wrote volumes about the flora of Assam. My grandmother opened a university for women and then died of pleurisy in the Himalayas. She was only thirty-eight. My parents crossed the Atlantic when I was two months old, and here I am. These snippets of knowledge are puzzle pieces strewn across a table, waiting to make a picture.

I peek into a bedroom through an open door. One thing about me—I can be nosy when nobody's around. There's a double bed between two nightstands. On the chest of drawers sits a large wood carving of a many-armed god with an elephant's head and a rotund belly. Plates filled with candy surround him. The elephant's round face is kind, caring. A glow of comfort infuses me. Staring into the jolly elephant face, I could swear that he is alive, watching me.

"Lord Ganesh," Dr. Ghose says from behind me, "Remover of Obstacles. Very fond of sweets. Consult him in times of difficulty, but be careful. He's a bit of a trickster. Always playing jokes."

I turn, heat rising in my cheeks. "I—was just looking for the washroom."

Dr. Ghose points down the hall and smiles.

MAYA IN THE MIDDLE

FIRST thing in the morning, we stand at our desks and sing the national anthem. I used to wing the verses:

> *O Canada,*
> *Our homeandnative land!*
> *True putrid love in all our sons command,*
> *With glowing hearts we see thee rice*
> *The True North strong and free!*
> *O Canada, we stand on guard,*
> *We stand on guard for thee.*

* * *

Pride surges through me for my True North, although I wonder what we stand on guard for and why it would matter if we did since an army could march right over a bunch of kids. I also wonder what *homeandnative* means, exactly. The song pops out of me anyway, as easy as zipping my parka.

Next we recite the Lord's Prayer. I know all the words, but secretly I like the pop-song version better. I know there's a Lord in Heaven named Hallowed, which is probably where Halloween comes from. I have no idea what *Forgive us our trespasses* means, and *Give us this day our daily bread* has to get boring. The same thing day in and day out, like Dad on his stir-fry supper kick last month when Mum first returned to university.

Next come French and music classes with Miss Barth, who in another life could've been an evil nurse. She smells of rubbing alcohol, and I suspect she would love to poke us with needles. She has long, copper-colored hair, and freckles. She wears brown mascara lumped on her lashes, miniskirts and platform shoes. She plays the piano and speaks in musical terms. "Never B flat, sometimes B sharp, but always B natural." I'm never B'ing natural enough. I monopolize conversations, don't pay attention and don't learn French phrases. I keep forgetting that *Il n'y a pas d'élève qui sache la réponse* means *There isn't a student who knows the answer.* According to Miss Barth, I don't live up to my Full Potential.

I wish for a blizzard to bury the streets in snow so I don't have to go to her class, but I have to see her on evenings and weekends too, when she teaches ballet at the community center.

Ms. Redburn, who teaches English and science, is the opposite of Miss Barth. I can do no wrong. Ms. Redburn reminds me of Teddy, a stuffed koala bear I lost in Winnipeg. Ms. Redburn has a huge mole on her left large cheek, a faint mustache, thick, black curly hair and a feathery voice. She likes to hug me. Her hug is like falling into marshmallows.

"Call me *Ms.* Redburn," she says. "Not Mrs. or Miss. *Ms.*"

She's into women's lib. Her WonderBra boobs poke holes through the air, and she makes us split into groups and do plays. Mine is *The Brementown Musicians.* I play Belemente Chanticleer, the rooster, and have to make a red comb out of cardboard and tie it to my head. My friend Sally Weston plays Songe the cat, while Psycho (nicknamed for her love of horror movies—her real name is Celia McCann) plays Chanter the donkey. Psycho resembles a donkey even without her costume.

The whole thing is embarrassing, teenagers acting in third-grade plays. Ms. Redburn would rather teach younger kids, but she's stuck with us.

I'm in the advanced class, but that doesn't help in the cafeteria when I find leftover rice and dahl in a Tupperware bowl in my lunch box. Mrs. Ghose's leftovers, a mushy mixture smelling of tamarind and coriander. I think of banyan leaves swaying in a wet monsoon wind. Not that I remember a real monsoon, but I can imagine one. Rain flying sideways, washing away heat and dust and leaving seething currents of black water swirling through the jungle.

Indians are made for jungles and monsoons, after all, aren't they? Someone told me that once, maybe the babysitter who moved to Saskatchewan. Dark people are made for jungles; white people are made for snow. I'm not sure what I'm made for, and I'm not sure how Indian leftovers got into my lunch box.

Now I remember—we were leaving last night, and Mrs. Ghose shoved a doggy bag onto Mum's lap as she got into the car. Funny how one minute I want nothing more than to understand Bengali, and the next I long to erase every trace of India. There's room for India at the Ghose house, but not at school with bullies closing in. Maybe I'll throw away the whole Tupperware bowl, lid and all. Kids glance over as they walk by, screwing up their noses as if passing an outhouse at summer camp.

Sally sits across from me. She still has Songe whiskers drawn around her nose. She reminds me of a cat with her spindly legs and wispy, Farrah Fawcett hair. Her left eye looks inward, as if there is a very important spot on her nose that must always be watched.

"You eating barf again?" She sniffs my food.

"You eating chocolate sandwiches again?" I ask. Sally makes me sick sometimes. She likes mayonnaise-and-chip sandwiches too.

"Barfy puke." She ignores my question.

"Barfi is an Indian sweet. This is rice and dahl."

"Barfy barfi, barfy dahl. I can't believe you eat that stuff."

"I can't believe you eat Aero bars for breakfast. C'mon, I'll trade you."

"No way. You never eat normal food." Sally pulls out an egg salad sandwich and a plastic cup of orange Tang.

I nearly gag at the sulfur stench. I don't like eggs. Sally loves them. Her mum makes eggs as a special treat for her—deviled eggs, scrambled eggs, eggs over easy and soft-boiled, the worst.

Eggs are as bad as having Indian leftovers lurking in my lunch box. What if Mum slipped in leftover pakoras? She hardly ever has time to make sandwiches.

I try not to look into my lunch box as Kathy Linton sits with us. Miss Popular. She has boobs and gleaming white teeth. A glittering Bee Gees T-shirt stretches across her chest, showing the outline of a real bra underneath. Sergio Valente jeans cling to her thighs. She has done something to her hair, curled the blond ringlets back on either side of her face, like ribbons crimped with a pair of scissors. I smell candy, then realize the scent comes from Kathy's lip gloss.

Drawn by the shiny beacon of Kathy's lips, Adam McLean sits next to me. I shift over, my chair scraping the floor. Looks are thrown around the room. We're all playing dodgeball with glances and nobody wants to get hit head-on. Adam stares at Kathy while Sally stares at Adam as if he's cuter than Andy Gibb.

Everyone unwraps cellophane and chews and sips drinks through straws and laughs and talks. They forget about my puky barf rice and dahl, for now.

I peer into my lunch box, where another lump of danger crouches in aluminum foil. Or maybe it's a sandwich. Hopeful, I unwrap the foil. Two doughy triangles of pastry stare up at me like foreign stowaways. Leftover pakoras. I think of Sahadev fishing a pakora from his glass, snorting milk out his nose. He would never survive here at Garfield School.

Brian Brower and his gang take over the next table. His gang never sits. They stake out territory and conquer.

"She's eating nigger food again," Brian says.

I freeze, the word *nigger* branded into my forehead, jumping on my brain. I imagine getting up, throwing rice and dahl in Brian's face. Splat. The dahl will drip down his hair. I will rub his nose in dahl. My mind thinks up ways to stand up and fight back, but my body stays sitting.

I swallow the bitter taste in my mouth.

Psycho throws Brian a murderous look. "Watch what you say around my friend."

I look at her. She can be surprising.

"That nigger is your friend?"

A few kids glance our way. Sally frowns and stares at her shoes.

17

"She is not a nigger. She's my friend." Psycho sips soup through a straw. "Don't you dare call her that ugly word."

I'm still staring at her. I want to say thank you, but a hard anger grips my throat. The words won't come.

"What do niggers eat, Marcus?" Brian asks the red-haired guy sitting across from him.

Marcus shrugs.

Please let this be over, I think. The Vacancy sign goes up inside me again.

Brian rummages for his lunch in a wrinkled brown paper bag and elbows the friend sitting next to him. They whisper and snicker.

There are no black people in our town, so I guess I'm the next best target. When I die, I'll become an exhibit at the local museum. *Mayasri Mukherjee, born in India to a Bengali father and an Anglo-Indian mother. Nobody knew exactly how to classify Maya, but we do know this: she was all mixed up.*

I am Nowhere Girl in my Nowhere Land, between Canada and India.

THE GIRL IN THE PICTURE

I stay late after school to color the cardboard costumes in Magic Marker, Chanter's tail and Chanticleer's red rooster comb. At four o'clock, everyone's gone but Ms. Redburn, who is reading *Ms.* magazine.

"Will you be okay by yourself?" She glances up for a moment.

"I am an independent woman," I say.

Ms. Redburn smiles.

Our town is safe. We have no crime, and I have never seen police.

I trudge home as twilight falls and the snow hangs heavy on the trees. There's a certain calm in walking alone. I don't have to try to be anyone, and the vacancy inside me fills with thoughts.

I'm reading *Are You There God? It's Me, Margaret.* Judy Blume knows the trouble with being my age. I'm not so sure about God. Although Dad's family is Hindu, he doesn't pray to or worship Hindu gods. He worships the universe and Einstein's theory of relativity. I make a mental note to find out how God fits into the laws of physics.

I wonder whether Mum's side of the family prays to God. Her Mum is British, blond and blue-eyed, a Product of the Raj. She married an Indian and lives in India and writes Bengali children's stories. She doesn't write about religion, and she doesn't talk about religion, although she warns me not to listen to the Jehovah's Witnesses when they come in their Sunday best to Save Us. From what? Brian Brower, the bully? That would be fine. He's been calling me names since he moved here from Edmonton last year. Dad says not to worry. I come from a country rich with culture, and Brian is merely envious. Still, I'm relieved to see no sign of him as I head for the post office.

This is my job every afternoon, to check our mail. Nobody in town has a real mailbox on their property. Sometimes I wish for one, the kind people have in the movies. They run down the driveway to the mailbox and dash back to the house, waving a letter from a boyfriend.

There is a boyfriend in my mind, and maybe the waiting inside me has partly to do with him. His name is Jamie Klassen, and he's fourteen. He yelled "Congratulations, professor" after I won the science fair three years in a row. If I brush past him at school or in the library, I can feel him looking at me, and not in a bad way, not the way Brian Brower looks.

Jamie stares as if he's been wandering through a desert for days and I'm tropical punch.

I don't tell anyone, not even Psycho, not even my diary. Well, I tell my diary in code. Sometimes I fill my mind with scenes of Jamie and me. We walk home together. He puts his arm around my shoulders. We make igloos or go tobogganing.

I open our post office box with the key and pull out the envelopes. We have bills from Manitoba Telephone and Marks and Spencer and a blue airmail envelope with a small photograph trapped inside—I can tell by the stiff feeling. It's from India, addressed to me!

I can't run home fast enough.

The letter is my personal India, not the Mrs. Ghose kind of India. The letter is my relatives reminding me they are there, waving from a distant shore. They haven't forgotten.

I bring the fragile paper to my nose and smell mango, spices, the scents of the ages, of my ancestors. I see a black, spidery script through the paper and the outline of the photograph, a head shot.

I run the rest of the way home, holding up the envelope to the fading light. I can't recognize the round handwriting. Usually, I can tell if the letter is from Thakur-dadu, my father's father, or from Cousin Joyantoni, or from my great-aunt who calls herself simply Auntie. She stands nearly a hundred feet tall in a sari with her long, silver hair flowing like the mythic hair of Shiva.

When I get home, the house is dark and silent. Mum and Dad won't be home for an hour yet. I turn on the desk lamp, throw off my parka and slide the opener carefully along the edge of the letter, so as not to cut through the writing.

The photograph falls out into my hand. I draw a sharp breath. The girl in the picture radiates fairy-tale beauty, every molecule molded just so. Her hair is night flowing rich and bold past her shoulders. Her wide Indian eyes are the brightest stars, her lips red and full. Her creamy skin—one could almost touch it—gives off a vibrant life. Suddenly, my fingers look plain. I remember the metal in my mouth. The sharp braces push at my tongue. The linoleum on the kitchen floor, the Formica countertops, the teacups left from this morning—everything turns gray, boring. The only mysterious element of life is this girl's smiling face.

Dearest Maya,

I hope the gods have kept you in good health and spirits. Forgive my irregular correspondence. I have been dancing Kathak, rowing for Modern High School and bored in general. My best friend, Sandhya, is on the opposite rowing team and now we do nothing but fight. I always win.

How are your classes? Auntie Kiki and Babi-Mama, are they well? Have you got a boyfriend? I hear that many girls in America have boyfriends quite young. This must be such freedom. Here, Ma suffocates me with her watchful eye.

You will keep this in confidence, between cousins. Do not tell anyone, all right?

I convinced Ma to let me study abroad. She wants to send me to London, God forbid. I would much rather stay with you, Maya. We could have such fun together as cousins. You must tell me all about the boys in America. Please tell Babi-Mama to ring up my ma for a chat.

Xoxoxoxoxoxoxoxoxo
Pinky

Pinky calls Mum by her childhood Bengali pet name, Kiki. Only very close friends and relatives say Kiki or call Dad by his pet name, Babi. My teachers, Dad's colleagues and formal acquaintances call Mum and Dad by their given names, Kamala and Amitav, which they use to sign applications or checks. It's strange to see Kiki, such an intimate name, in Pinky's handwriting. At least she didn't write *Dear Maya-baby* or *Dear Bumpy*, my pet name as a baby. Before my body was ready to sit up, I kept trying, bumping my skull against the crib until a lump formed on my head.

Pinky's given name is Priyanka, but she always signs her letters Pinky. I don't know how she can get America and Canada mixed up, but I'll set her straight.

She has become way too beautiful.

PLASTIC BUBBLE

WE'RE having one of Dad's stir-fry disasters for supper.
He mixed canned pineapple and mandarin orange slices
with red-hot chili peppers and Brussels sprouts, a deadly
combination. At least he did not boil eggs.

My parents eat in silence, while outside, dandruff
snowflakes flit down in the darkness. I wait, pushing the
food around on my plate. I asked whether Pinky could
come, and Mum said we would *discuss the issue*.

I imagine Pinky and me staying up late every night, a
permanent sleepover party. We'll use flashlights under

the blankets and read romance novels to each other: *His sardonic gaze stripped her naked.*

Mum will let me wear lip gloss and kohl. Maybe Pinky and I will go on a double date. The buddy system. Maybe I can get my hair feathered or cut in a wedge.

"She'll be a good influence," I say, munching my Brussels sprouts. I'm careful not to drop anything on the place mat or clink my fork on the plate. I keep my elbows off the table and eat with my mouth closed. These are the rules.

"It's too bloody cold here in winter," Mum says. "Pinky won't last a week."

Every Christmas we fly south like Canadian geese— to Barbados, Trinidad or Antigua on vacation. Maybe the Caribbean islands remind Mum of India. They give me a heat rash.

"Winter is the best!" I say. "Tobogganing, cross-country skiing. Making snowmen. Throwing snowballs. She could even go skating." I slide my gaze toward Dad.

He chews slowly. "The flight is expensive, Maya-baby."

"Auntie can pay. She wants Pinky to study abroad. Either here or London." I spit the word *London* with disdain, the way I imagine Pinky might speak. I picture the city as a polluted hole full of soot and disease.

Mum and Dad keep chomping, biding their time.

"She needs to learn proper English," I add, "maybe French too."

"London, eh?" Dad grabs a Brussels sprout from my plate and pops it into his mouth.

"Dad! Come on." I pretend to protest, though his habit of stealing my supper is useful when I don't like the food. "She prefers Canada. Can she come?"

Mum frowns. "I don't think it's a good idea. You need to focus on school."

"Pinky can help me focus."

Why is it so hard to get my parents to say yes? Our home is hermetically sealed. The Family in the Plastic Bubble.

"Maybe next year, Maya-baby," Dad says.

I focus on what he once told me—I have always been stubborn, strong-willed. When I banged my head against the crib in an effort to sit up, I tried until I succeeded.

"Next year will be too late. Pinky will end up in London," I shout.

"Perhaps in the spring or summer." Dad steals a mandarin orange slice from my plate.

"Well, we may not be here in summer." Mum throws Dad a knowing glance.

"Why not? Why wouldn't we be here?" My voice rises.

Dad raises his eyebrows at Mum.

She places her fork carefully on the plate. "You like going on holiday, don't you, Maya?"

"I'd rather have Pinky come here."

Dad clears his throat. "How would you like warm

weather all year, to be able to go to the beach every day . . . ?"

Didn't he hear anything I said?

"I'd rather turn into Frosty the Snowman."

Mum arranges and rearranges the knife and fork on her plate. "In a few days, a real estate agent is coming to show us some photos of houses in California. Would you like to have a look?"

I shake my head. "What houses? I like our house. This house is perfectly fine. Pinky will love staying here."

I get up, shove my chair back and carry my plate to the kitchen. Why are my parents talking about real estate agents and going to the beach every day, when all I want is a visit from Pinky?

I spend the next hour being perfect. I wash all the dishes, dry them and stack them just so, wipe down the table, finish my homework in record time.

"We could study together," I say to Mum and Dad, reading in the family room. "And cook."

"We'll see," Mum says.

We'll see is better than no but not as good as yes.

At night, murmuring voices drift from the conference chamber, the master bedroom. My parents flip the idea upside down, check underneath, hold the pros and cons up to the light.

I frustrate myself into restless dreams. Mum and Dad are walking ahead of me on a beach. I fall behind, boiling in my parka and boots. My parents grow smaller and smaller until they disappear and I'm standing alone in the blazing sun.

In the morning, I wake up sweating.

Mum comes in and says she is doing me this huge favor. Pinky can stay for a few weeks.

"The rules won't change. You mustn't stay up until all hours."

I agree.

"Or make a mess, or stay at friends' houses on school nights."

I promise.

"You must do your homework."

Of course, I say, I'll do my homework days early.

She snatches a pair of balled-up white socks from the floor. "Honestly. One minute I've tidied your room, the next minute a hurricane strikes."

I'll clean my room before it gets dirty, I say.

Mum seems satisfied, for now.

＊ ＊ ＊

Dad calls his elder sister, Pinky's mum, at eight o'clock in the evening.

"Have I woken you, *Didi*?" he yells, his voice echoing through the house. *Didi* means sister. He covers one ear with the palm of one hand and presses the receiver to his other ear. "What time is it there? What? Breakfast? Hah, breakfast?"

I picture the crackling telephone lines racing east across Manitoba, Ontario, Quebec, New Brunswick, Nova Scotia, dropping into the Atlantic Ocean and swimming across to Europe, then hiking through Iran and Pakistan and finally to India.

I sit on the couch and flip through the *Winnipeg Free Press*, pretend to read while Dad asks after his father and cousins, aunts and uncles. I can't concentrate on the Archie comics.

Finally, Dad shouts, "Listen, *Didi*, we're expecting Pinky to come. For studies here? Pinky! Maya is quite excited. Hah, hah. Of course. No problem."

There's a long pause. Dad nods, listening. I imagine the continents rising between him and his closest sister, now separated by an unfathomable distance. The seconds tick by, filled with static.

Dad does the sideways head nod. "Hah, good, good," he shouts. Good what? I'm on the edge of my seat. "Tell her to bring warm clothes. Nah, not a shawl. Very warm clothes. Like Darjeeling. Snow, *Didi*!"

When Dad hangs up, change is afoot. Cousin Pinky will arrive in exactly one week.

A lot can happen in a week.

GOOD TOES, BAD TOES

MISS Barth has us doing kid stuff in ballet.

"Good toes, bad toes. Good toes, bad toes!" she yells above the Bach invention blaring from speakers on the gymnasium wall. She walks with her toes turned outward, legs straight, shoulders back.

I sit in the second row, my legs stretched ahead, toes pointing forward for good, up for bad. *When she was good, she was very very good. When she was bad, she was horrid.* I think of Cousin Pinky dancing Kathak and being "bored in general," as she wrote in her letter.

"Maya. Keep in time," Miss Barth yells. "Eyes forward, shoulders back. Sally Weston, Kathy Linton. You too."

I find the rhythm again.

"Up we get, girls! Pirouette. Focus on one spot on the wall. Eyes forward, turn, then snap your head around."

My pirouette unravels like yarn out of control, but I stop before bumping into Kathy Linton. She spins in place, prima-ballerina perfect. Sally tips over and rights herself like a Weeble toy. *Weebles wobble but they don't fall down.*

"Come to the barre. Hop to it." Miss Barth claps, and we rush to the wooden barre against the wall.

"First position, second position." Miss Barth strides back and forth, tapping a hip here, a knee there. "Stand up. Don't slouch. Bottom in. Stomach in. Chest out." She raises her arms, and I can't help staring at the dark copper tufts in her armpits. A glimpse into the hairy world of grown-ups.

"And one, and two," she booms.

I feel a current of air coming from the doorway. I have a strange sixth sense, knowing someone important is standing there. Sometimes teenage boys who hang out in the pinball room walk over to watch the "little girls" take ballet. The leotard stretches tight across my chest, and my ballet slippers stick out like clown shoes.

Without turning to look, I close my lips over the

metal junkyard in my mouth. Whoever stands in the doorway isn't leaving. I can't help turning just a little.

Oh no. I whip my head forward again. Careful, don't turn around. Don't slip. Don't mess up. Jamie Klassen is leaning in the doorway.

Invisible hands grab my ribs and squeeze. What is he doing here? Jamie is tall and way too cool in his muscle T-shirt, open bomber jacket, jeans and combat boots. So cool his breath turns air to ice. He's the wild boy with the gray eyes and the John Travolta strut, who skips school and gets suspended for smoking. He knows who I am, gives me that thirsty-in-the-desert look.

I'm doing ballet positions at the barre in my leotard with my underpants riding up. With my arm out to the side, in second position, I can't adjust my underwear.

"Mayasri Mukherjee, tummy in, chest out!" Miss Barth screams.

Fire lights my cheeks. I'll burn to ash and blow away. Why does Miss Barth have to say my full name, "Mayo-Scary"? She can't even pronounce the words. Not even the Romper Room lady on TV could pronounce my name; she never saw me in the Magic Mirror.

"Miss Mukherjee, are we distracted today?" Miss Barth shouts.

The fire spreads—I must look like a turnip or a beet. A turnipy beet. A turnipy red beet with my underpants riding up.

My foot slides back from second position to third. I

press my lips shut to hide my braces, take a deep breath. Jamie Klassen is still standing there. I can feel him. Another part of me, the show-off, thinks, Fine, if he wants a show, I will give him one. I watch myself as if in a dream as the spotlight captures me in glittering tutu and tights.

I glide onstage and curtsy. The audience stands in a roar of applause. I push off from the barre, leap in a pas de chat, "step of the cat." More clapping. What am I doing? This isn't me. Part of me stays behind, watching in horror while my show-off self takes a running start, pirouettes, then slips and lands hard on my tailbone.

I am on the floor.

"Mayasri Mukherjee. What on earth are you doing?" Miss Barth hoists me up by my armpits. The room spins.

The girls giggle as I stagger back to the barre.

"Did you hear me say pirouette?" Miss Barth yells.

The empty doorway tilts in my wavering vision. The music clicks off. What have I done?

The girls let go of the barre.

My tailbone throbs, but I don't care. Everyone gets ready to leave. Jamie is gone. When he sees me walking home, he will pretend he doesn't notice me. I've ruined my chances forever.

Sally tries to talk to me on the way out, but I ignore her. I would rather sulk all the way home through the blistering snowstorm. If only I could crawl down into the tundra and join the mini-fossils millions of years old. Imprints of fish scales and lizard bones.

"Maya, wait up." Sally comes running from behind, breathing loudly in the cold.

I slow down.

Sally catches up and breaks into a Farrah Fawcett smile.

"If you keep your eye on one spot as you pirouette, you won't fall," she says.

"I know. Thanks." Like you did a perfect pirouette, I'm thinking. *Weebles wobble but they don't fall down.*

"I saw Jamie Klassen," Sally says with wonder, the way Mrs. Ghose sounded when she found out I couldn't speak Bengali.

"Yeah, so?"

"He likes you."

"No way. How do you know?" An ember of hope flares inside me. Sally calls my food barfy, and she gossips, but I like her.

"The way he looks at you. The look of a crush."

I know the look she's talking about.

"He asked about you," she says.

"You're lying!" But my feet lift off the ground. I float.

"No lie," Sally says.

Now I stop on the snowbank where we are walking and stare at her with my mouth open. "What did he say? When?"

"He lives down the street from me. I always see him. He asked where you live and what you do."

"What do you mean, what I do?"

Sally sighs, as if I'm a dunce. "How do you think he ended up watching you at ballet?"

"You told him about ballet?"

Sally shrugs. "He might be waiting near Kinsey House."

A SMILE TO DIE FOR

I walk on top of the snowbank to avoid cars sliding by, wheels spinning on ice. With each step, I get closer to Kinsey House, to Jamie Klassen. Except he might not even be there after seeing me fall. He probably changed his mind. A klutz isn't worth the trouble.

I take the sharp right turn into the Kinsey House hotel parking lot, dotted with cars wearing hats of snow. I angle right toward the field, the shortcut home.

Jamie's there.

He leans against the wall. My stomach flips.

He smiles, pushes off the wall to walk with me.

"What's up, professor?"

His voice is deeper than John Travolta's.

I can't speak.

Our boots crunch through the snow.

"You're good at that spinning-around thing," Jamie says. He's even taller up close.

My heart beats so fast I can't keep up. He has to be joking. Maybe I could believe him if he said I was good at playing piano or waxing my cross-country skis.

But pirouettes?

"Thanks," I say.

"Do you ever do Indian dancing?"

Where did that come from?

"No."

"Ever wear a dot like your mom?" he asks, shoving his hands in the pockets of his bomber jacket.

"What dot?"

"On the forehead. What does it mean?"

"Just a decoration." I turn to look at his profile, but he is already turned toward me and our gazes collide, bam. Gray eyes, and he is smiling. A smile to die for.

"So you never wear a dot?" Tiny ice crystals form on Jamie's nose. *Rudolph the Red-Nosed Reindeer had a very shiny nose.*

"Not me." I wear Chiquita banana stickers on my forehead. No bindis.

"You'd look good with a dot," Jamie says. "Purple, or maybe green."

"Giant green booger on my forehead? They don't come in green." I think of Dad picking his nose. Oh no. Why did I say *that*?

"What colors do they come in?"

"Red. My mom uses lipstick, presses it on her forehead."

"Do you ever wear Indian clothes?" he asks.

"I'm not really Indian." Only adults wear saris. Grown-up women whose bodies are worlds complete with hills, valleys and mysterious folds of skin on their stomachs.

If Jamie walks any closer, I'll faint.

"So you want to be a ballerina?" he asks.

"Nah, I'm going to be a writer." Where did that come from? I've only told Anne Frank in my diary.

"Groovy." He nods.

We reach the end of Kinsey House field. He walks me to my driveway. Our house is dark. Dad and Mum aren't home yet.

"Why don't you come over tomorrow, after school?" Jamie says. "I'll show you my records."

As I nod, my heart marches ahead to tomorrow.

A lot can happen in a week.

EAU DE JOY

FOR now, the house belongs to me. When the grown-ups are gone, the rules relax and walk around in their underwear. I lock the front door, peel off my outside clothes and run to the hallway mirror. My cheeks are flushed. My eyes are shining. Do my braces show? Do I have a booger in my nose? Is there a spot on my fore-head where a bindi should go? I'm not thinking about Cousin Pinky or the Ghoses or Brian the bully. They all file into my blind spot while my mind whirls around Jamie Klassen.

My friends have crushes on him, but he wants *me* to listen to records before his father gets home tomorrow. Too much is happening too fast.

Tomorrow, Mum gets home earlier from the university. I'll have to make up a story to explain where I'm going after school.

First, I need lip gloss. Bonne Bell. I wish I could get my hair cut and feathered, but Mum won't let me yet. I need Joy or Chanel. I tiptoe into my parents' bedroom. Where's the perfume?

I check the nightstand on Dad's side. Lamp resting on a lace doily. A paperback novel and a bottle of antacid tablets. On the bottom shelf, more books. When I open the drawer, a chaos of mail bursts out. Bills, letters.

A photograph is mixed in with the mail. Dad is wearing a white Indian kurta pajama, drinking whisky and smoking a cigarette, his mouth half open. Instantly, I imagine him lecturing. That's what he does at the plant or while traveling. A lecture in Amsterdam, in Palo Alto, in Washington.

Rifling through the drawer, I feel vaguely guilty for trespassing. Nickels and dimes have fallen to the bottom. Dad leaves change everywhere, in piles straight from his pocket. He doesn't keep track of details like coins, safety pins, or stories I've written for him. His mind reaches out to travel at the speed of light.

Dad is a hip version of Einstein without the frizzy white hair or wrinkles. He drinks Glenlivet, smokes sweet-smelling pipes, listens to *Hair* the Broadway musical, goes to parties. Dad is one of a kind.

Indianness is also rubbed into him like permanent dye. He taps his fingers to ragas, wears Kolapuri chappal sandals and drinks Darjeeling tea brimming with milk.

I pick up a few nickels—picture of a beaver—and a quarter—picture of a caribou. The old Canadian folk song comes into my head: *Land of the silver birch, home of the beaver, where still the mighty moose wanders at will. Blue lake and rocky shore, I will return once more. Boom di di boom boom, boom di di boom boom, boo-oo-oom.*

Instead of "O Canada," I would much rather sing this beautiful folk song in class. The sweet tune brings an ache to my heart. This is my home.

Why does the land of the silver birch come with bullies? While I'm wishing Brian Brower away, an image of jolly Lord Ganesh, the elephant-headed god I saw at the Ghoses' house, pops into my mind, just like that. He is watching me.

I close Dad's drawer and hurry to Mum's side. Identical nightstand, only much neater. Thermometer, bottle of Bufferin and folded tissues in the drawer. Lotion. Paperback mystery on the bottom shelf. Mum is a mystery encrypted in those pages.

I pick up the paperback, and a brochure falls out. A photograph of a white-sand beach with aquamarine water. A business card is stapled to the bottom. *Mike Armstrong, Realtor,* address in Santa Barbara. Did he come all the way from California? I remember what Mum said about him, then push the thought out into the snow.

I put everything away and check one more place. I find the Joy perfume in Mum's underwear drawer. I'll use some tomorrow.

When my parents get home, I lie about tomorrow, tell them I'm going to Psycho's house to do homework.

"Be good," Mum says. "Don't watch TV, and say please and thank you."

I promise, cross my heart.

THE MAPLE LEAF
CHRONICLES

"WHAT if your mom calls and asks for you?" Psycho walks close to me on the way to school. This morning is extra cold. My thermometer is the frozen snot on her upper lip.

"Say I'm in the washroom." I kick a block of gray snow.

"What if she calls again?"

"Say I had to go really bad."

"If she calls at four, then at five, you're still in the washroom?"

"She never gets home before five. I'll be home soon after that."

Psycho scratches her orange eyebrows growing together into one caterpillar line. "Why don't you and Jamie come over to my house? We could stay up late and watch a horror movie on TV."

I think about this for a minute. I imagine grabbing Jamie's arm at the scary part, and Jamie holding me. But not at Psycho's house. "Your sisters will be home, and your mother too!"

"They're always home, so what?" Psycho is the youngest of four. Her sisters practice putting on mascara, lipstick and nail polish. Psycho prefers blood, guts and rolling in the dirt.

"Jamie invited me to his room, in his empty house," I say. "It will be just him and me."

"Maybe we could watch *The Exorcist*. Linda Blair vomits that green stuff straight across the room, and—"

"Ew, Psycho. I'm going to throw up."

She grins at me. "Then her head spins all the way around and makes this crackling sound—"

"Stop!" I think of how I had to turn my head nearly all the way around to get my parents from no to yes.

"You could sleep over." Psycho raises her one long eyebrow.

"I'm not allowed to sleep over anywhere on school nights." Then I remember—Pinky is coming! How will I divide my time between her and Jamie? Life gets complicated, but I'll find a way.

At lunch, I am dead.

How can we still have Indian leftovers? Mum must've frozen Mrs. Ghose's samosas and sneaked them into my lunch box.

I should've checked. Now Kathy and Sally and Psycho sit at my table, and Brian and his gang stake out their territory. Only this time, as I'm about to throw away the samosas and go hungry for the rest of the day, Jamie saunters in with a tray of macaroni and cheese. His friends don't follow him.

He plunks down his tray and sits right next to me. You couldn't fit a hair between us.

"Hey, professor, how's it going?" I can feel the heat rising from him.

"Hi, Jamie," Psycho and Kathy say in an awed chorus.

Sally stares at Jamie's black bomber jacket and slicked-back hair. Half-chewed peanut butter and bread nearly fall out of her mouth.

"Hey, Jamie. I heard you got the best Gordie Howe card for sale," Adam says. He is sitting on the other side of me, staring across the table at Kathy Linton. "The signed one, collector's edition."

"Not for sale." Jamie picks up a samosa and turns it around, examining the pastry from all angles. "Is this Indian food?"

The table falls silent. I can hear my own shallow breathing.

"Yeah, it's a samosa," I whisper.

Silence.

"Cool," Jamie says. "Trade you."

Everyone watches him slide his macaroni and cheese over as he devours the samosas in a few bites.

"Hey, these are good."

"You like them?" Samosas *are* good. Brian Brower should taste them. I am no longer dead at lunch.

"Yeah," Jamie says, then more softly. "See you later?"

I nod, anticipation making the words stick in my throat.

The only thing better than eating samosas is watching Jamie Klassen eat samosas.

❋ ❋ ❋

The afternoon slides by so slowly.

In English class, Ms. Redburn has us reading ghost stories, although we are past Halloween. We're discussing "The Monkey's Paw" by W. W. Jacobs, about a shriveled paw that had a spell put on it by a fakir, an Indian holy man. The paw could grant three wishes each to three separate men.

"Observations?" Ms. Redburn paces, stroking the fuzz on her upper lip. "What is the moral of the story?"

We are all comatose from lunch. Usually, we would rather put our heads down and nap, but today I'm way too excited.

Sally's hand shoots up. "Don't *ever* wish on a paw from India, or you're in big trouble!"

Ms. Redburn turns and writes Sally's comment on the blackboard in round words.

"Anyone else?" She turns around, a dab of white chalk on her nose.

Psycho's hand goes up. "Don't be greedy and wish for money, because your son might get mutilated in machinery and then you'll get the company money, and then if you wish for him back, he'll rise from his grave all mangled and bloody, with his arm hanging off, his eyeballs on a string, his guts spilling out everywhere and—"

"We get the picture. What does this tell us?"

The bell rings then, and we are saved.

I traipse around the whole school, but there is no sign of Jamie.

After recess we practice *The Brementown Musicians*. Psycho keeps forgetting her lines. Half the time, all she has to do is bray. She's a donkey. She has just come across me, Chanticleer, in the road when Ms. Redburn calls me to her office.

" 'If You Could Only See It My Way,' " she says, handing back my writing assignment. "This is original, Maya. The way a blade of grass views the world." She smiles and I smile back at her faint mustache. I don't say I wrote the story in five minutes. It isn't that good. I chose grass because I couldn't think of anything else.

"I have an idea." Ms. Redburn rummages in her desk and pulls out a magazine, *The Maple Leaf Chronicles*. "I thought you might like to read this."

"Homework?" I take the magazine. On the glossy cover, watercolor maple leaves catch fire in yellow, orange and red. *Autumn Issue, Volume X* is printed in the bottom right-hand corner.

"No, it's not homework. Maybe you could send your story to the editor." She gives me a marshmallow hug.

"My story? No way!"

"Think about it."

Why would the editor of such a beautiful magazine print my silly story about a blade of grass? I'll add this to the list of things I can't do: speak Bengali, do pirouettes and send my stupid story to an editor.

It doesn't matter. I'm going to Jamie's after school.

FRAGILE

STEPPING into Jamie's bedroom, I lose my breath. My heartbeat pulses out into the warmth. I'm here, where he sleeps. If the girls at school knew, they would faint.

He switches on a dim overhead light. Not exactly what I expected. Quilt on a single bed and a chest of drawers. Brown shag carpet. The curtains half closed. At home, Mum yanks open the curtains. She hates any room dark or closed. There must always be light.

Jamie doesn't have a mum here. She is alive, but she ran away. The worst. So he decorated his own room, I can tell. Night sky spreads across the ceiling painted cobalt blue. Posters plaster the walls, no space in between. Colors and faces, crowded and clamoring, connected by Scotch-tape corners. The Six Million Dollar Man from TV leans forward, running bionically with one eyebrow raised, the Farrah Fawcett swimsuit poster right next to him.

Minus ten points for Jamie.

"I can't believe you have that." I am not amused.

"Have what?" Jamie kneels in front of a shelf packed with records. A black comb sticks up from his jeans pocket.

"Farrah Fawcett. You have a crush on her?"

"It was in one of Psycho's magazines. *Tiger Beat* or something. No biggie." Jamie shrugs, but his ears redden.

"No biggie." My voice must sound wrong, because Jamie glances at me.

"You have a crush on the Six Million Dollar Man." His eyes darken to gray twilight.

"I do not. How do you know?"

"Sally Weston told me."

"She talks too much." I wonder if Sally told Jamie about us playing bionics, running in slow motion, hurling Nerf balls and pretending they're five-hundred-pound boulders. I could die of embarrassment.

"What's that smell?" he asks.

"What smell?"

"Are you wearing perfume?"

"It's Joy." Did I pour on too much?

"I like it a lot."

Relief!

"I want you to hear something." He pats the bed.

I nearly wipe out on my way to sitting down. So close, I can see the veins and muscles in Jamie's arms, the tiny brown hairs all growing in one direction.

The wall below the window is a shelf packed with albums.

He slides a record from its jacket and holds the vinyl disk between thumb and forefinger, like holding butterfly wings. He puts the record on the turntable and places the headphones over my ears. His fresh-soap smell comes closer.

He looks at me with expectation, one hand on the stereo volume. I guess he loves this music.

"I can't hear anything yet." My voice sounds muffled, distant.

Then one note reaches into both ears at once, an electric tone that pushes louder and louder and then just when I'm sure my head will explode, the tone pulls back and switches to acoustic guitar. A deeper bass rhythm moves underneath, complex and mathematical.

I'm in a dream, floating to a mountaintop on words strange and cool. *Call it morning driving through the sound and in and out the valley* . . . This isn't Donna Summer or Heatwave's *Too Hot to Handle*. This is Bach woven into metal music sweeping me away.

Jamie's eyes glint. How can this music even exist if I haven't imagined it?

When the song is over he pulls off the headphones.

"Amazing, huh?" he says. "It's called 'Roundabout.' "

"It's like my dreams of flying."

Jamie moves closer on the bed to show me the album cover. YES in big round letters on a blue background with the round earth painted bright green. The album is *Fragile*.

That's the way I feel right now, fragile, with Jamie's leg touching mine, the weight of his arm around my shoulders. I am human Jell-O as Jamie tilts my chin up with his hand and kisses the corner of my mouth. His skin is dry and cool, and I can taste his breath. Then he lets go, leaving the tingling imprint of his lips on mine. I'm a snowflake melting in his warmth.

"You taste good," he says.

"Good 'n' Plenty," I say, and then the front door slams. I didn't hear the car. There is movement downstairs.

My heart races. Jamie looks at me. His eyes widen. He stands up and lifts the quilt. "Get under the bed."

"What about my boots?"

He grabs my Cougar boots and shoves them under, my parka too. His glance goes wild around the room. He shoves everything under the bed with me and then, only a moment later, the door opens.

"Water all up the stairs, all over the damned carpet." Jamie's father.

The stench of stale beer hits my nose.

"Sorry, Dad." Jamie tries to sound nonchalant, like flipping hair. Only I hear the fear running underneath.

I hate being under here with the dust bunnies. There could be spiders or worse. Plus I feel sick, hiding like this. I want to jump out, pop up and tell Mr. Klassen we were just being teenagers.

"What did I tell you about mess? Huh? Answer me."

"Dad, it's water."

"Think I like getting my socks soaked?" Mr. Klassen's voice gets louder. I hold my breath. Maybe Jamie's dad can hear my breathing or smell the Joy perfume.

"I said sorry, Dad. What the hell more do you want from me?"

"Goddamn it, don't you ever talk to me that way."

There's a silence, then footsteps stomping away. Jamie sits on the bed above me. I sense him gathering himself. I should not have heard this.

Finally, he peers under the bed and whispers, "You have to go."

I scramble out and brush off my jeans, pull on my parka and boots as fast as I can, shaky and strange.

"Will you be okay?" I whisper.

"I'm peachy. Now get out of here."

"I can't believe he yelled at you over stupid water."

"Yeah, well, he's crazy. But he's my father." Jamie peers out into the hall and then ushers me in front of him. How does he know it's safe now? Then I hear the shower in his dad's bedroom and someone whistling "American Pie."

Outside, I break into a run. How can a square bungalow look so normal and quiet on the outside and be so unpredictable on the inside? I guess Jamie doesn't like it either, so he hides in the world of Yes, *Fragile*.

MUSIC LESSON

HORROR.

Vishnu Ghose, the great god who is everywhere, comes over in his high-water polyester pants and snow boots to take piano lessons after school. I did not agree to this, and I don't know why Miss Barth doesn't teach him. She teaches me every two weeks, and yells at me for not living up to my Full Potential, as usual.

So what if I prefer practicing folk songs—"Careless Love" or "Santa Lucia"—or disco hits instead of silly sonatinas from the Royal Con-stuffy-tory of Music?

I get a meager allowance, a dime or a quarter thrown like a bone whenever I sit with Vishnu, who has onion breath and likes to dig for earwax. He and Dad would make a great team—the nose picker and the earwax digger.

I try to teach Vishnu simple tunes from *Christmas Carols for Beginners,* only Christmas will arrive before he learns "Good King Wenceslas," and he only has to use one finger.

He fidgets on the piano bench, his gaze everywhere but on the keys, and makes smacking noises with his lips. I know he would rather be playing Pong, and I would rather be with Jamie Klassen.

Mum and Dad come home in the middle of the piano lesson. They bring a stranger with them. A stocky, bald man wearing glasses so thick, he could see the craters on Mars through the lenses.

"Maya, this is Mike Armstrong." Dad stamps snow off his boots.

I freeze, my hand halfway to turning the page in the music book. I remember the brochure in Mum's nightstand. "Shouldn't you be in Santa Barbara? Don't you live there?"

"Maya!" Mum gives me a warning look. Oh no. She'll know I snooped.

Mr. Armstrong nods and smiles. "I'm just back visiting my son. The wife and I used to live here, but we couldn't take the cold."

"I love the cold," I say.

"You'll love Santa Barbara too. The white-sand beaches look just like snow."

Sand and snow are not the same, I'm thinking. I shrug, pretending not to care, but the music book slides off the piano, and I accidentally put it back upside down and on the wrong page.

COUSINS TOGETHER

PINKY stands six inches taller than my five feet zero. She brings the heavy scent of Yves St. Laurent Opium perfume and half of India in her Samsonite suitcase. On the way home from the Winnipeg airport, she lounges beside me in the Chevy's backseat, her slim legs crossed. She's a glittering star in bangles, jewels, and a turquoise sari. Her shiny eyes take up most of her face, and she drowns in a fall of black hair. Beneath that woolen coat and choli, she has boobs.

I disappear inside myself, a clumsy kid. It's hard to believe Pinky and I are related.

"How are you liking your studies?" she asks. Her "are" comes out *"ahhh,"* a breath.

"Who, me?" I point stupidly at myself. "Oh, you mean school. It's fine."

"Your maths? You're studying calculus already, nah?"

"Oh no. I'm learning algebra. How about you?" Indians don't say Englishes or Frenches or Latins. But they say maths.

"I don't bother much with studies. I want to become a model in *Star* magazine," Pinky says, stroking her hair. "In Bombay, where all the models and actresses live."

How can I top that?

"Maya will become an astronomer or perhaps a physicist," Dad yells from the front seat. "Nobel Prize material."

Oh no, not this.

Pinky makes a face at me, and I shake my head.

"I'm going to be a writer, Dad."

"I saw your nice story about grass. Now I'm reading, what is it?" Dad says, "the *Leaf* magazine—"

"The Maple Leaf Chronicles," Mum says.

"Acha. Chronicles."

"Ms. Redburn gave me that magazine, Dad. In case I want to send them a story."

"Very nice," Dad says. "But you must be practical!"

"I'm too young to be practical." How could Dad take my *Maple Leaf Chronicles* without asking?

Pinky studies me. "If you are to become a famous writer, you'll need a snap for the book cover, nah? We must pluck our eyebrows and—"

"I'm too young to pluck my eyebrows."

She touches her upper lip and gives me a knowing look. "We are never too young to remove unsightly hair."

I wonder how she plans to do this. Light peach fuzz grows on my upper lip, but nothing like Ms. Redburn's mustache.

Pinky flips one of my ponytails. "You need a much more grown-up style as well. Don't you think so, Auntie Kiki?"

"Feathered, maybe? Or a wedge?" I'm hopeful.

Pinky raises her curved brows and nods.

"Your hair is fine," Mum says.

"Wait until you're much older," Dad says over his shoulder.

"You are quite old enough for change, nah?" Pinky winks.

"She's right. I'm ready for a new hairdo. What if I die before I get older? I should feather my hair while I have the chance. Can I?"

Pinky grins at me, and I grin back.

"We'll see," Mum says.

"Next thing she'll want to go out on dates with boys," Dad grumbles.

Pinky sticks out her tongue at the back of his head. I hold up two fingers, rabbit ears behind his seat, and Pinky and I break into silent laughter.

We are cousins together.

THE GOLDEN GOD

MY parents go shopping, leaving Pinky and me alone. In the washroom, she arranges hairbrush, toothpaste, toothbrush, comb, earrings and Opium on the counter. She leaves no room for my things, which are piled in the medicine cabinet.

Then she turns the guest room into her territory. Maybelline lipstick tubes litter the dressing table. Her coat hangs over the armchair in a haze of perfume. She drags her suitcase onto the bed, while I sit on the mattress with my legs dangling.

"This is so exciting, to be here in America!" she exclaims.

"Canada is not the same as America," I say. "Manitoba is just north of Minnesota and North Dakota."

She flings open her suitcase with a theatrical flourish. India whirls upward like a genie in silk, incense, churidar kurtas, sandalwood oils and the medicinal scent of Pears soap.

She gives me a small perfume bottle with a gold cap. I unscrew the cap and sniff. "Wow—Chantilly!" I have wanted this. I dab on the scent. Jamie won't say *What's that smell.* He'll think this is my natural scent of roses.

"You are sophisticated. Cosmopolitan." Pinky tilts her head sideways.

Cosmopolitan? I peer into the full-length mirror. I see a skinny brown girl with limp ponytails, braces and two zits on her nose. Oh! That's me.

"For Auntie Kiki." Pinky unfolds a shimmering blue sari with a gold pattern woven along the hem. "And for Babi-Mama." Kolapuri chappal sandals and a white cotton kurta pajama for Dad.

"And for your classmates." She lines up miniature sandalwood elephants on the bedspread.

Classmates? She must mean my friends.

Then she unwraps a statue of sitting Ganesh made of gold. Although he is only six inches high, the wisdom of the universe resides in his elephant face. His diamond eyes radiate light from a thousand suns. He has only four hands, but each commands galaxies. One hand is free, palm outward in a gesture of peace. His right ear flops forward a little.

A craving pulls at my insides. I hold my breath, hoping Pinky will give him to me.

She places him on the chest of drawers, presses the palms of her hands together and bows her head. Her lips move in silent prayer.

"Where did you get him?"

Pinky stops praying and looks up at me. "He's been in our family for generations. Your father's side, the side we share." She points at his hands. "See—one holds an axe made of his broken tusk, one a lotus flower and the other a conch shell. Sometimes he holds a rosary."

Bathed in the serene light of this golden Ganesh, happiness blooms inside me, a field of daffodils in winter.

"Why do you keep him in here?"

"Ganesh is everywhere in India, adorning storefronts and homes, on T-shirts and handbags. He sits at the mouth of all temples, the first god prayed to before undertaking any task. Ganesh grants wishes and removes obstacles. He is a most beloved and benevolent god."

"What do you pray for?" I think of the many-armed Ganesh in the Ghoses' bedroom.

"Great riches! I *must* have a green brocade silk sari from the Paus Mela or the Chowringhee bazaar."

I imagine Pinky kneeling in front of an elephant and

praying for a sari from the "Poosh May-la," whatever that is. I know a bazaar is a bunch of Indian shops squished together, like a mall.

"How did he end up with an elephant's head?"

Pinky touches his trunk. "To know this, you must know how Ganesh was born."

"He had a Mum and Dad?" I can't imagine a god being born.

Pinky nods. "His parents were the great god Shiva and the goddess Parvati. Shiva loved to meditate. Once, while he was away, Parvati grew lonely, so she molded a son from clay and breathed life into him.

"She asked him to stand guard at the door while she bathed, and not let anyone in. When Shiva returned, the boy would not let him pass. In a fit of rage, Shiva lopped off the boy's head.

"Parvati rushed out and screamed in horror. When she told Shiva that he'd killed his son, he wept and rode out in search of the boy's head, which had been thrown a great distance.

"In the forest, an old elephant crossed Shiva's path and offered his own head. Shiva thanked him and set his spirit free, so that the elephant's soul could fly to join the *devas*, the gods.

"With the elephant's head, the boy returned to life. Parvati made him leader of the *ganas*, her followers, and named him Ganesh, her son."

I feel sorry for the elephant who gave up his head, but I suppose he's happy living with the gods.

"Can I keep him in my room for a while?" I ask.

Pinky gives me a look as if I've asked for her soul. "I really don't know—"

"I promise to give him back. I have a lot of questions for him. Please!"

"For a day or two, perhaps."

I grab Ganesh with both hands. He's heavier than I expected. He must be solid gold. I rush to my room and place him on my chest of drawers. Rummaging through my desk, I find a box of Jelly Bellies left over from Halloween and arrange them by flavor in a circle around him: Very Cherry, Lemon, Cream Soda, Tangerine, Green Apple, Root Beer, Grape and Licorice.

"I hope these are good enough for you." I lean forward and press my hands together in the prayer position. "Dear Ganesh, since you're a god, maybe you could explain how gods fit into the laws of physics. Gods know everything, right? So why am I the only brown kid in my school? Are there lots of other Indian kids in Winnipeg, or Toronto or Ottawa? You're from India, so you see Indian kids all the time, and I bet nobody calls them niggers.

"Anyway, I want to live happily ever after with Jamie Klassen. He doesn't seem to notice my zits, but could you please get rid of them? You're the Remover of Obstacles."

I spend the next half hour confiding in Ganesh, and soon I begin to feel he's a trusted friend. My room buzzes with a new energy. Magic shimmers in the air, or maybe it's only the afternoon sun.

NAIR GIRLS

PINKY bursts into my room without knocking. She's waving a pink bottle with a chemical smell. "See what I've brought for removing unsightly hair!"

"What are you doing?" I can't help staring at Pinky's face. A thick, white lather coats her upper lip.

"Come on, you must try. I'll put it on for you, nah?" She's a ventriloquist barely moving her lips.

A red warning sign flashes in my mind. Pinky has been cooped up too long in India. She might go wild here in the True North.

She drags me to the washroom and leans close to the mirror. "Our skin will be smooth as silk."

My ghost of a mustache isn't noticeable. Mum doesn't have a mustache, and I've never seen her use Nair. She might do so in secret. I wonder how Ms. Redburn would look without her mustache. Marshmallow pretty.

I sit on the toilet seat and let Pinky smear Nair on my upper lip. The cream is cold and stings. Besides our blood, what else about Pinky is related to me? Not the way she walks in long strides, shoulders thrown back. Not her dramatic voice and gestures. Not her huge eyes or rich hair. The nose that wrinkles when she concentrates? I can't tell. I don't watch my own nose.

"There. Now you will be beautiful." She steps back to survey her work.

"How long do we keep it on?"

She reads the instructions on the bottle. "At least four minutes."

"Our lips will be smooth?"

"You expect a boy to want you if you are covered with hair?"

My cheeks heat up. She does not know about Jamie. Did my mini-mustache tickle his lip?

"My skin is burning," I say. "How much longer?"

"Just another couple of minutes. Let us pluck our eyebrows."

She must see the horror in my expression.

"It is not painful." Pinky rummages in her toilet bag

and produces a pair of giant tweezers. "Look at yourself. Your eyebrows are growing together. How do you expect to get a boyfriend with a single eyebrow?"

Jamie doesn't seem to mind my eyebrows.

"They haven't merged yet," I say, but now my flaws glare at me in the mirror. Bushy brow, zits, braces and hairy cream-covered upper lip.

Pinky's eyebrows form perfect arcs above her perfect eyes.

I sit on the toilet and let her pluck at my forehead. It hurts a little, but not as much as my burning upper lip.

When she's finished, my brows have gone on a crash diet. They are two skinny threads above my eyes.

"Did you take off too much?" I frown.

Pinky huffs indignantly. "Absolutely not. I have done you a world of good."

I'm not so sure, but it is too late now as the garage door rattles open and the Chevy rumbles in.

"Quick!" I say. "We have to wash off the cream."

Pinky's eyes widen. She slams the door and presses the lock on the doorknob, then sprays a cloud of Opium into the air, making me cough.

Footsteps in the hall. Bags rustling.

"Girls?" Mum knocks on the door. "What are you up to in there?"

"Nothing," I say in a casual voice. "Pinky's just showing me her bindis."

"What's that awful smell?"

Pinky spritzes more perfume into the haze.

"New perfume, Mum! Pinky found it in the duty-free shop."

"Not a very nice scent, is it? Don't be long. We're having supper soon."

Footsteps fade down the hall.

We break into giggles of relief and quickly wash off the Nair.

My upper lip feels smooth against my fingers.

The only problem is, my skin has turned red. Pinky's skin is neon pink.

"Oh, Shiva!" She scratches her lip. "What's happened?"

"It burns and itches." I try not to scratch, but this is worse than poison ivy. "Maybe we waited too long. You were too busy plucking my eyebrows off."

"Thinning them!"

We stand in front of the mirror, and I see a family resemblance between us. We are two Nair girls with skinny eyebrows and identical pink skin rashes.

YESCANDY

BY Sunday afternoon our skin rashes fade. Psycho and Sally show up to see the New Cousin from India. In my room, they swoon over the statue of Ganesh and bombard Pinky with questions. What was it like to fly in a plane by herself? What is sandalwood? Why does she smudge charcoal around her eyes?

Kohl or *kajal*, not charcoal, Pinky explains.

What is a vegetarium?

Vegetarian, Pinky says. I don't eat animals.

Why?

One day, she says, I was walking through a Bombay

bazaar when I came upon the carcasses of lambs and calves hanging upside down. The horror of those dead eyes struck me so hard, I stopped eating meat from that moment forward.

Oh wow, my friends say in unison.

Why do you wrap yourself in a bedsheet? Psycho asks.

It is not a bedsheet. It is a sari, Pinky explains.

I try to picture Psycho in a sari. All I can see is a donkey draped in silk.

Pinky demonstrates, first putting on a long white petticoat tied at the waist with a drawstring. Then she folds the end of a turquoise sari into the petticoat and wraps the fabric once around. She makes seven pleats in the sari, tucks them in, wraps the rest of the sari around her waist and brings the end up over her left shoulder. When she finishes, my brain is tied in knots. I'll never remember all the wraps and tucks and pleats.

A vision in blue, she twirls in front of the mirror in my bedroom, then shows us Kathak dancing. Precise finger movements, coy smile and bright eyes flashing. She stamps her bare feet on the floor and spins around and around, faster and faster. Then, bam, she is still.

"You should dance for the town!" Sally shouts, her left eye staring at the spot on her nose.

"Yeah, at the community center," Psycho says.

I say nothing, remembering my ill-fated pirouette.

"What an extraordinary idea! I shall speak to Auntie Kiki," Pinky exclaims.

Speak to Auntie Kiki?

Pinky sits cross-legged on the bunk bed and runs her fingers through her long, black hair, so shiny and dazzling that we will all go blind without sunglasses.

"When you dance, do you wear the dot on your forehead?" Sally asks.

Pinky nods.

"Maya, how come you don't wear the dot?" Psycho turns to me. "Or a sari? How come you don't speak Hindu?"

"Hindi, not Hindu," I say crossly. "And it's not even Hindi. It's Bengali. India has hundreds of languages."

"How come you don't speak it?" Psycho insists.

Speak *it*? Hasn't she heard a word I said?

"Yeah, you're Hindi!" Sally blinks at me as if I'm a munchkin from the land of Oz.

My face heats up. "Hindu! *Du!* And I'm not."

"Perhaps her parents want to help her become fully American," Pinky says in a serious tone.

"Canadian," I say. I wonder if what she says is true. Do my parents expect me to fit in better speaking only English?

"Do you have a boyfriend?" Psycho asks Pinky. The dancing and Hindi are already forgotten.

"Probably ten or twenty," Sally says.

"No boyfriend, but I plan to have one here." Pinky puffs out her chest, making her boobs even bigger.

"How can you *plan* to have a boyfriend?" Psycho asks, wiping her nose, which is always running. "I sent Adam McLean twenty-six valentines last year, but he ignored me."

"You need to act more like a *girl*," Sally says. "Learn how to make good sandwiches—"

I laugh. "Boys don't care if you make sandwiches."

"Sally still toasts chocolate sandwiches in her Easy-Bake Oven," Psycho says.

Sally sticks out her bottom lip. "Adam *likes* my sandwiches. I gave him one at recess last week. He ate it all."

"Such freedom, to give chocolate sandwiches to boys at recess," Pinky says. "We can't do such things in my all-girls school. Do you also go out on dates to see films in dark theaters?"

"Fil-ums?" Psycho mimics Pinky's pronunciation.

"She means movies," Sally says.

"Do you kiss the boys, like this?" Pinky puckers her lips.

I think of Jamie's lips on the corner of my mouth.

"We'll ask the Ouija who Pinky will kiss," Sally says. She opens my closet without asking and pulls out the Ouija board. My books slide off the shelves. We have books everywhere. Books on the family room shelf, lined up on the mantelpiece. Cookbooks in the kitchen, boxes of books in the basement.

Sally sets up the Ouija on the carpet, and the four of us sit in a square around the board.

Psycho shows Pinky how to rest her fingers on the message indicator. Our hands are all different. Sally's fingers are long, with blond hairs. Psycho has pudgy fingers with dirt under the nails. Silver rings adorn Pinky's delicate fingers painted with a golden tan.

My fingers are boring brown.

"Now concentrate," Sally says. "Don't press down."

We concentrate. Nothing.

"Is it broken?" Pinky asks.

"Ouija, tell us who Pinky will kiss," Sally says.

The message indicator doesn't move. Maybe the Ouija doesn't care who Pinky kisses. He has more important topics on his mind, like saving the world.

"This is boring," I say. "We have to call a spirit."

"I'm calling Attila the Hun," Psycho says.

Sally coughs. "No bad guys. Charlie Chaplin?"

"How about a writer?" I say.

"Farley Mowat," Psycho says.

"He's still alive," I say. Doesn't she know anything?

"Pierre Trudeau," Sally says.

He is not a writer, but how would Sally know since she reads only the Bazooka Joe comics inside bubble-gum wrappers.

"He is still your prime minister," Pinky says. "Which means he is probably alive as well."

We all look at her. If she knows the name of our prime minister, she must know we're in Canada and not America.

She shrugs. "I read the *Statesman*."

"My aunt Gretchen, then," Psycho says.

Sally rolls her eyes. "Not your aunt Gretchen again. The meanest aunt who ever lived, even meaner. Saying she was mean doesn't even go halfway to how mean she was—"

"How about an Indian god?" I say, glancing at the golden statue of Ganesh on my chest of drawers.

"Chief Sitting Bull!" Psycho says.

I expect her to bat her mouth with her palm and hop around like the Indians in Westerns.

"Not that kind of Indian. *India* Indian," I shout. I am sick of explaining the difference.

"Come to us, India Indian," Psycho says. Her orange eyelashes flutter shut.

I keep one eye open, watching Ganesh. "Tell us your name, O Indian god." I make my voice deep and hypnotic.

Again, nothing.

"Speak to us, O god," Sally chants.

"Maybe we should have a séance instead," I say.

Pinky looks at me. "What is a séance?"

"We call the dead with candles." Psycho rubs snot from her nose.

Pinky's eyes get so big and shiny, I can see my reflection distorted in her pupils.

"The Ouija works better," Sally says. "O god, please show yourself."

"Not show," I say. "Speak, through the board."

"Speak through the board, O god," Sally says. "There aren't any Indian gods here."

The indicator begins to move, slowly at first, in a sweeping circle.

"Oh, Shiva! It's alive!" Pinky lifts her fingers. The indicator stops moving.

Sally snorts with laughter. "Keep your fingers on there."

Pinky puts her fingers back on. If we're not the ones moving the Ouija board with our subconscious minds, then the indicator should move without our fingers, only

it never does. Psycho says that's because our bodies chan-
nel the spirits, but I'm not so sure.

The indicator takes off again, to the letter *S*.

"*W*," Psycho says with excitement.

"*E*," Sally says breathlessly.

"*E*," Pinky says.

"It already went to *E*," I say. The indicator moves at
high speed. *T*, and *S*.

"*S-W-E-E-T-S*," I say.

"Sweets?" Psycho frowns.

"Candies," I say.

Sally's brows furrow. "*Sweets* is candy? There's a spirit
ghost named Candy?"

"You're moving it," Psycho says.

"My fingers were barely on," Sally says. "Pinky, were
you moving it?"

Pinky shakes her head. "You saw."

"I wasn't moving it either," I say.

"Then what does *sweets* mean?" Psycho asks.

"I don't know. Kind of scary." Sally pushes a strand of
blond hair behind her ear.

We try again, and this time the indicator rushes
around to YESCANDY. I think of Yes, *Fragile*, and an
ache comes to my heart.

We all lift our fingers. The indicator stops moving. A
breath of wind touches the back of my neck, although
the windows are closed. The statue of Ganesh is still in
its place, motionless on my chest of drawers.

GANDOO

MONDAY morning, Pinky begs to wear my clothes to school, so I give her my old Levi's, the ones I wear weeding the garden in summer.

Pinky wriggles into the jeans, then poses in front of the full-length mirror in my room.

"Sexy, nah?" She puts her hands on her hips and does a little jig. "Ma would have a fit. How do I look?"

In my stained, sky blue Levi's, Pinky looks good. Better than good. The jeans look like royal Levi's tailored for Princess Pinky.

"Maybe you'd better try on a different pair," I say.

"But these are brilliant." Pinky pushes a strand of hair behind her ear. "How do I look? American?"

I know she knows the difference.

"You mean Canadian. No, you still look Indian."

"Oh, Shiva!" Pinky spouts a stream of Bengali, which reminds me that she doesn't even think in English. "I want a typically Canadian shirt!"

"Molson Canadian, a moose, a beaver or a big maple leaf? I don't have anything typically Canadian."

She throws me a hurt look.

I choose a pale blue peasant shirt that doesn't fit me properly. When I stretch my arms, it feels as though the shirt will rip in the armpits.

The shirt hangs on Pinky just right. Desperation tugs at my insides. It's nearly time for school, I'm not even dressed yet, and Pinky is already perfect.

The worst of it comes when she tries on my extra parka. It fits her better than it fits me, and it looks even better on her than it looks on me, and then Mum hands us two lunch boxes and pushes us both out into the snow.

At school, my friends gather around Perfect Pinky, who will dance at the community center this weekend. Mum arranged the performance to broaden the town's cultural horizons.

Pinky mesmerizes the teachers. She knows the answer to every question.

At recess, she wants to make a snowman in the

schoolyard. The air turns icy and there's no wind; snowflakes flutter down like tiny white butterflies. I show Pinky how to roll a snowball for the head. Psycho and Sally traipse off to find twigs for the hair.

Then Brian approaches and stops a few feet away. Melting snow seeps between my gloves and the cuffs of my parka. My wrists are numb.

"Is that your nigger cousin?" he asks, staring at Pinky.

She hoists the head onto the snowman and straightens up. She looks like an angry princess. "What did you call me?"

A knot tightens in my stomach.

"Is she half nigger and half white, or what?"

"We—are—not—niggers," I say, my voice wavering. "Don't *ever* use that word about anyone."

"How come her skin is lighter than yours?" Brian glares at me, his eyes narrowed.

Pinky's eyebrows knit into a furious line. "What's the matter with this idiotic boy? *Shoo-or ka bachha.*"

"What kinda language is that?" Brian shoves his hands into his parka pockets and steps back. He looks uncomfortable.

"Gandoo!" Pinky points at him. Then she bursts into laughter.

Brian gapes. Maybe he thinks Pinky put a curse on him. He turns and walks away, breaking into a run as he nears the school.

Sally and Psycho return with bundles of twigs.

"What's wrong with you two?" Psycho shoves sticks into the snowman's head.

I tell them what happened.

Sally blinks the way she does when the teacher calls on her in class, and her left eye turns farther inward.

Psycho kicks a clump of snow and wipes her nose.

"What is this word, *nigger*?" Pinky asks, waving her arm in a grand gesture.

"You don't want to know. It's cruel. Wrong," I say as we all trudge back to the school.

Pinky falls into stride beside me. "Cruel like the insult I gave him?" She breaks into easy laughter. "I called him a son of a pig and a hermaphrodite."

I smile a little, but Brian's words are poison in my stomach. "Crueler than the other name he used to call me: Chocolate Face."

"You look more like toffee," Sally says, inspecting my nose.

Psycho whacks her in the arm. "You don't get it! Who cares what she looks like? Brian is mean. He called me Fatso and Jelly Roll."

"Jelly Roll?" Sally giggles.

"It's not funny. Nobody ever called you names. You won't know what it feels like until it happens to you."

I stare at Psycho. "He called you Fatso?"

"Yeah, it hurt. He thought he was so funny."

"Why don't you tell the teacher about him?" Pinky asks. "Brian should be punished."

Psycho frowns. "I wish he would go away."

"Me too," I say. "I wish he would move to the North Pole."

"Why? Are you ashamed?" Pinky stares at me.

"Why would I be ashamed? I'm perfectly fine." The heat creeps to my cheeks. Maybe Pinky's right. When Brian calls me names, I don't want anyone to know. I want to stuff his taunts into a garbage bag and throw them away.

Pinky squares her shoulders. "Brian knows nothing about you. He doesn't know our family. Our grandmother wrote books. Our grandfather studied in Europe and fought for India's independence. He knew the great Mahatma Gandhi."

"Wow, Gandhi!" Psycho says. "I bet Brian's family never met anyone famous."

"Brian has a narrow mind." Pinky speaks in a grown-up voice. "Don't let his words affect how you feel."

I try to absorb her confidence. I try to remember that I come from a country rich with culture. I try to forget Brian's words, but my heart still flutters and my legs feel like rubber.

LUMP OF NOTHING

JAMIE is home with the flu. The waiting inside me grows, an ache for the One. I don't see him all week, until Pinky's Kathak performance at the community center.

She leaves three hours early to practice and primp backstage. The rest of us pick up free tickets at the door and get our hands stamped with a blue maple leaf.

I'm a string bean in a faded green churidar kurta borrowed from Pinky. *Don't you look smashing!* she lied. The pant cuffs drag in the snow, and the long shirt billows, meant for Pinky's mountainous boobs. This must be the old kurta she wears around the house.

At least I get to wear my hair down, the next best thing to getting a wedge cut. I'm a touch exotic with my tresses flowing. I rub kohl on my eyelids, but I refuse to wear the bindi. A few things I will not do, and pressing a bloodshot eyeball blotch on my forehead is one of them.

It's bad enough that I have to file in with the small crowd of Pinky fans, mostly our friends, and sit next to my parents in the third row. Dad wears his usual corduroy, while Mum's blue silk sari rustles and sways.

I scan the crowd for Jamie. The Ghoses arrive in fancy Indian garb. Tonight, the boys' plaid high-water nerd pants are spanking new.

Then Jamie pops out of nowhere and sits right next to me. I hold my breath, Yes, *Fragile* racing across my skin. His scent drifts into my brain. He nods, a trace of knowing in those gray eyes.

I give him a faint smile, the best I can do, considering my insides are jiggling Jell-O.

"You look pretty with your hair down." He touches a strand, and the back of his hand brushes my cheek.

I beam, a heat inside me.

"Dr. M, Mrs. M." Jamie nods over my head at my parents. He is so polite.

"Where's your father?" Dad asks.

Jamie gives me another look. "Working."

On a case of Molson Canadian, I am thinking.

If my parents knew about Jamie and me, they would have heart attacks and die.

"Maya, Maya!" Sally rushes up in a fluffy dress bursting

out beneath her parka. She's a bouncing lace doily with blond curls. She points to the back of the auditorium. "We're sitting in the last row! Come on!"

"I have to sit with my parents," I say, and Jamie and I exchange grown-up looks. Still, I can't help glancing back over my shoulder. Psycho and Kathy wave and smile.

"How come you're not going to dance, Maya?" Sally says.

"I do ballet, not Kathak." I'm already shrinking into a mouse scurrying along between chair legs, dodging boots.

Sally smooths her dress. "You're Indian. Why don't you just get up there and dance?"

My fingers itch to strangle Sally and put her out of her doily misery, and then Jamie says, "Hey, Sal—go on back, the show's about to start."

Sally's mouth drops open, astounded that Jamie spoke to her directly. Flustered, she flounces back to her row.

Jamie and I roll our eyes at each other. He is Mighty Mouse come to save the day.

As the lights dim, I catch a glimpse of Miss Barth and Ms. Redburn a few rows ahead. Brian Brower and his family are not here, and I can think of others who didn't come tonight.

Jamie and I sit next to each other in an intimate darkness. I stay perfectly still, my elbows touching neither Mum on my left nor Jamie on my right.

After what seems like a hundred years, the curtain rises and Pinky glides onstage. The first things I notice are the silver bells around her ankles. She glitters in red, gold and silver all over, and a shiny black braid swings as she takes slow, exaggerated steps, nodding her head.

Mum leans over to whisper. "The invocation to the gods."

I imagine an invocation to Ganesh's rotund belly.

Pinky gestures, strikes a sitting posture in the air. Her bright star eyes widen in mock innocence as her arm extends.

"She's telling a story," Mum says. "That's what *katha* means. Story. A Kathak is a storyteller. She's the new bride sitting on her bed as she prepares for the night. Now she reaches for the candle, snuffs it out . . ."

Pinky snaps her hand back.

". . . and burns her fingers."

Pinky shakes her hand. Drums crackle over the loud-speaker. She stands, moves faster, stamps her feet. The bells jingle as she stomps, swirls, slaps her feet on the wooden stage, faster and faster until her movements blur. It's a frightening, elegant performance. I sit perfectly still, taking in the ethereal beauty of Pinky, absorbing her Indianness.

There is a subtle change in Jamie. He has not moved, but everything about him leans forward.

I grip the edge of my seat. The golden statue of Ganesh dances into my mind. Remover of Obstacles, Granter of Wishes. I wish for the dance to be over, for Pinky to be gone.

The dance doesn't end. It's one of those infinite events, like an evening raga, stretching for hours, days or years. Pinky's ankle bells jingle faster and faster as she stomps and twirls—bang bang bang.

Then the music fades.

The audience claps and whistles. Pinky smiles shyly and wipes the sweat from her forehead. Her chest heaves beneath a dozen gold necklaces. Then she leaves the stage, stepping backward on her heels with her henna-covered toes pointed upward, hands clasped in front of her as if she's praying.

The audience gives her a standing ovation. I stay sitting while Jamie leaps to his feet. The people in front of me block my view but who cares.

"Wow," Jamie says.

"Lovely, lovely," Dad says, grinning and shaking his head.

"Wasn't she marvelous?" Mum exclaims as the lights come on.

What an act, I am thinking.

Out in the hall, kids clamor for Pinky's autograph. I nearly fall in the crush. Jamie rushes through the throng, waving a bandana for Pinky to sign.

I don't get a chance to talk to him before my parents whisk me out into the Chevy. Pinky jumps in beside me.

I sit in stony silence, and just before Dad guns the engine, someone bangs on the door.

Mum rolls down her window. Jamie pokes his head in, his cheeks flushed. My heart leaps.

"Dr. and Mrs. M?" he says breathlessly. "Can I get a ride home?"

"Hop in the back," Dad says.

I hesitate, then open the door and slide closer to Pinky, which I would rather not do, but what choice do I have when the One wants to get in next to me?

Jamie folds into the car, his gangly legs and arms all over the place. His jeans touch the length of my leg, sending a shiver through me.

"Thanks, Dr. M," he says. "I appreciate the ride."

Dad revs the engine and the Chevy bumps along the snowy road. Jamie's bomber jacket is unzipped at ten degrees below zero.

"You were good," he says over my head to Pinky. "The dance was groovy. Way out. Thanks for the autograph."

What am I? An armrest?

"You are very welcome, and you are very kind." Pinky's voice flutters.

"She has to wear cowbells on her ankles," I say.

"They are not cowbells. The proper name is *ghunghrus*," Pinky says. "Considerable skill is required to use them."

"You're very skilled," Jamie says. "How long are you staying?"

"Not long," I say.

"Maya!" Mum says.

Dad turns up the radio volume as he swings onto Burrows Road and whistles off-key to "No Time" by the Guess Who.

I stick out my elbow, putting space between Pinky and me.

"I do so love Canada," she says to Jamie. "Perhaps I'll stay forever." So she does know the difference between Canada and America!

Jamie grins.

"My parents would not let you stay forever," I say. My braces cut into my tongue.

Dad and Mum can't hear. They're lost in the Guess Who.

"Auntie Kiki said I may stay as long as I wish," Pinky says.

"What?" She's lying.

"You'll love springtime," Jamie says, "when the daffodils and tulips bloom. Farmers grow all kinds of crops—wheat, corn and barley. To the north, on the tundra, the soil is permanently frozen underneath. It's called permafrost. Did you know Manitoba is bigger than Japan and twice the size of the United Kingdom—"

"She's from India, not Mars!" I shout. I've never heard Jamie talk so much.

He gives me a perplexed look.

"I do so love the snow," Pinky says. "I would very much like to make an igloo."

Oh, right!

"Igloos are easy," Jamie says. "I could show you how. Keeps you warm if you get caught in a blizzard."

Caught in a blizzard?

"I'd love to learn," Pinky says. "And go tobogganing."

"I'll take you," Jamie says. "Kids use Krazy Karpets. They're big sheets made out of plastic, with handles on the ends. I use a shovel. Works better."

The hair stands up on my neck. If Pinky goes sledding with Jamie, I'll give her our heavy wooden toboggan, the slow one that takes an hour to slide down the hill. I wish for her to wipe out on the way down, maybe crash into a silver birch tree and break her perfect nose.

"Come over after school," Jamie says. "I'll show you how."

"We have homework," I say.

"There will be plenty of time for homework in the evening, nah?" Pinky puts on the innocence.

Jamie gives her his thirsty-in-the-desert look.

A lump grows in my throat. I can't speak. I'll run away and live in a real igloo with the Inuit.

PRINCESS PINKY

WHEN I wake up, my throat is parched. Hot, dry air blasts up through the floor vents. Someone has turned up the heat to tropical levels.

Last night rushes back to me, and my stomach sinks. Jamie giving Pinky the thirsty look. Saying he will make igloos and go tobogganing with her. Pinky giggling and batting her lashes. She hypnotized Jamie with her Kathak moves, with the bindi on her forehead, with her sharp Indian accent and stories.

She told of evil rickshaw-wallah demons that eat

children in the Himalayas. You can tell they are demons by looking at their feet. Their toes point backward. I half expected Pinky's toes to turn backward.

Then Dad chimed in and said he had actually seen a rickshaw-wallah demon at boarding school in Darjeeling. He narrowly escaped by pretending to be a grown-up, tricking the demon.

Jamie kept asking questions all the way to his house. He said good-bye to Pinky, but forgot about me.

I can't believe I fought to bring Pinky to Canada. I worked so hard to bring my parents from no to yes, and for a little while, Pinky and I were mustache-rash cousins together. I felt as though I had a sister. Now I wish she would disappear.

In the family room, I find her arranged on the couch in a flowing cotton kurta. A different kurta every day. The room reeks of Opium. That perfume must be permanently soaked into her skin.

Mum is in the kitchen, making tea. "Pinky brought Darjeeling, First Flush. A highly potent blend."

All I can think of is First Flushing Pinky down the toilet. I sip tea strong enough to carry me to India. Mum added too much sugar. She adds either too much or too little.

"The dance was a great success, nah?" Pinky tilts her head, halfway between a nod and a shake.

A sour feeling curdles in my stomach.

"You were lovely in the kurta, Maya," she goes on.

"Would you like to wear a sari? I usually pack my extra saris for the needy, but what a good idea it was to bring them."

"What a good idea," Mum agrees, and takes her tea down the hall to get ready for university.

If Pinky gives me a donation for the needy, I'll accidentally flush the sari down with the First Flush.

At school on Monday, my friends praise Pinky's dancing. The girls gather around, asking her questions, touching her hair. She shines so brightly, even Brian Brower is blinded.

After school, I stay to help Ms. Redburn decorate the classroom for Christmas, which is still three weeks away. We paste cutout Christmas trees on construction paper and hang wreaths on the walls.

I would rather be here than watching Pinky and Jamie build igloos together.

"I'm sorry to hear you're leaving." Ms. Redburn is hanging streamers in the doorway to the cloakroom.

A bottle of Elmer's glue slips from my fingers and hits the tile floor. White liquid oozes out in a puddle. I bend to pick up the bottle. Glue clings to my fingers. Images of the Santa Barbara brochure and Mr. Armstrong, Realtor, burn into my mind. I can't ignore them any longer.

"I don't want to move," I say. "Dad has a great job here. He's director of the plant."

"Your mother wants to teach physics, Maya. She can pursue her goals in California."

"I wish she could teach here."

"We have few opportunities for advancement in this tiny town."

"Who needs opportunities?" I imagine the opportunity demons jabbing sharp forks into my life. But all I want is Pinky gone and to stay in my True North and live forever with the One of my dreams in Yes, *Fragile*.

Panic rises in my throat.

"Moving is hard, Maya, but you'll make the best of it." Ms. Redburn comes over to give me a marshmallow hug, then rests her hands on my shoulders. "Are you okay?"

I nod, although I'm not okay. I'm standing in a pool of glue. I'm destined for California, where opportunities lie in wait with their demon toes pointing backward.

My fingers come unstuck. The glue isn't strong enough to hold, and my longing isn't strong enough to fight the power of my parents. The power of *no*.

I stomp into the cloakroom, throw on my parka and boots and grab my schoolbag. Ms. Redburn's gentle voice drifts into my ear as I dash out into the hall. "Maya, wait! I want to help. If you need someone to talk to, I'm here."

I'm outside running in the dark and the quickening wind. Winter stars spread across the sky, and to the north, Polaris glints from a distance.

I know this sky, its shades of overlapping blue. I've memorized its patterns, the wisps of the northern lights. From here, I can't see the colors in the aurora borealis, only the white funnels against the night.

I know the crab apple trees, the weeping willows, the

Manitoba maple trees. I know the layout of streets, the flow of the Winnipeg River, the rustle of bulrushes in summer. I know the Canadian geese, the blueberries, the shapes of moss and lichen, the sour-sweet taste of rhubarb.

We can't be moving.

At the bottom of Burrows Road, I glimpse Jamie and Pinky several yards ahead, trudging toward Jamie's house. They hunch forward against the gale, their parkas touching at the shoulders. If they walk any closer together, their legs will get tangled.

They don't see me. I pull up my parka hood and follow.

Jamie stops at his driveway, standing so close to Pinky they could trade breaths. She giggles and flips her fall of black hair.

I hide behind a blue spruce tree. The cold climbs into my brain as Pinky stands on tiptoe and gives Jamie a kiss on the mouth. He steps back but doesn't protest.

My lips go numb as Pinky and Jamie stare at each other, then part ways. Jamie goes inside and Pinky hurries home. I will stand here forever and become one with the snow.

REMOVER OF OBSTACLES

MUM doesn't get home from the university in time for supper, so smoke hovers in the kitchen as Dad burns his latest science project—a mushy mixture of broccoli, carrots, macaroni, nuts and a horrible combination of nutmeg, cinnamon and cardamom.

Pinky cleans her plate as if this failed experiment is the best meal she has ever tasted. Her cheeks glow with guilt. I bet she's thinking of Jamie. Maybe he invited her to listen to records. Maybe she's making a plan.

I slip my supper onto a napkin in my lap, although

Dad has already stolen half the food from my plate. I roll up the napkin and throw the whole mess into the garbage. Then I run and shut myself in my bedroom.

I carry Ganesh into the closet for privacy, clear a space for him next to my shoes. Then I sit cross-legged and press the palms of my hands together. A tear slides to the end of my nose, plops onto Ganesh's golden head and trickles down his trunk. Help me remove obstacles. Remove Pinky. Help me stay in my True North, without Brian Brower. Make Jamie love me again. Protect me from Dad's supper experiments.

I spill all my problems to Ganesh, then arrange more candy around him so he won't go hungry.

As if he will eat.

I've outgrown the tooth fairy, Santa Claus and believing in magic, yet there is a certain comfort in knowing Ganesh has enough sweets. He doesn't care if I become a Nobel Prize–winning physicist, and he doesn't tell me to keep my elbows off the table or eat with my mouth closed. He doesn't care if I have zits or braces or skinny eyebrows that went on a crash diet. He doesn't force me to move to California. He doesn't pretend to love me and then betray me.

I rest my elbows on my knees, cheeks in the palms of my hands, and study the shape of his elephant head, the way his right ear flops forward. My inside self curls into the Vacancy, where a lonely wind blows.

I remember Jamie peppering me with questions on the way home from ballet. Why don't I wear a dot on my forehead? Indian clothes? A sari? Because I'm not Indian, not really.

Pinky radiates India from every pore. She doesn't have to try. Her country is mapped in her soul, tattooed on her skin.

Pinky is India.

I add this to the list of things I can't do: speak Bengali, do perfect pirouettes or be Indian for Jamie Klassen.

✳ ✳ ✳

I jolt awake in darkness. My clock radio flashes 4:00 a.m., 4:00 a.m., then 4:01, 4:01. A blizzard roars outside like a furious troll. The wind rages and howls; ice pummels the roof. A chewing sound comes from the closet. I sit up in the darkness, heart thumping. A mouse?

"Pinky? Is that you?" No answer.

I tiptoe to the closet. The chewing grows louder as I approach. A faint glow emanates from beneath the door.

I knock softly. "Pinky? Are you in there?" I imagine her sitting in front of Ganesh, stuffing her face with candy.

"No, it's me," says a miniature, tinny voice. "Have you got more Jelly Bellies?"

"Pinky, if this is a joke, it's not funny," I whisper.

"Pinky is asleep," says the voice. "Can't you hear?"

On cue, whistles and snorts drift from the guest room.

I open the closet door, flick the switch and squint in the harsh light until my eyes adjust.

The golden statue of Ganesh is busy munching. He

has demolished most of the candy. Bits of sugar stick to the gold around his mouth.

I rub my eyes, blink.

"This is a dream." I jump up and down and pinch my arms, squeeze my eyes shut and open them. I don't wake up.

Ganesh keeps eating, trunk swaying, four arms shoveling candy into his mouth.

"What flavor is this one? Licorice. Delightful."

I try to scream for Mum, but an invisible force sucks the words away.

"Come in and close the door. No use waking the whole house," Ganesh says.

I close the door and sit. I'm going to faint.

The gold takes on a fluid quality, moving easily at the joints of Ganesh's four arms. His eyes glint with life, though I can't determine their color. They seem to be made of light.

"I'm going crazy," I say. "Loony tunes."

"Are these all the sweets you've got?"

"You'll ruin your teeth if you eat any more—oh, what am I saying?"

Ganesh leans forward, peering over his belly, then, "No *gulab-jamin? Roshagola? Modaka,* sweet dumplings?"

"Mrs. Ghose makes the Indian sweets. We don't have any."

Ganesh's cheeks droop with disappointment. His trunk swishes. "Then we ought to get down to business."

I can't place his faint foreign accent. Maybe Indian, maybe not.

"Business? What do you mean? You're a statue." I pinch my arm again. I'm still not waking up.

"Gold, which rather limits my movements, but the icon is merely a vehicle. I am available in clay, carved wood or brass, reading or reclining, seated or dancing, surrounded by skulls—"

"Wait." I hold up my hands. "You're telling me I'm not dreaming?"

He nods, ears flapping.

"You arrived in Pinky's suitcase!"

"Indeed, and became quite ill with motion sickness. All that jumping and bumping around."

"But . . . you're an inanimate object! How can you feel motion sickness? How can you talk?"

"You summoned me. Now I am here."

"But . . . I'm not a Hindu."

"Hindu, schmindu. I don't discriminate."

"You can't be real."

"You called me with your Ouija board. You talk to me while picking your toenail or your nose—"

"Only Dad picks his nose! I have to get Mum—"

"I would advise against that."

"Why?"

"She will see what she can see, which means she will see a statue."

"She can't see you?"

Ganesh shakes his head. "Nobody else can see or hear me as I am now, talking to you."

"You really are Ganesh?"

He sighs. "I have many names. Akhuratha, One Who Has Mouse as His Charioteer; Anantachidrupamayam, Infinite and Consciousness Personified—"

"You're an elephant with a potbelly, if you'll excuse my saying so."

Ganesh nods. "What can I say? I'd be perfectly happy with Dumbo."

"You would not. Dumbo is a cartoon."

"True, and I'm not particularly fond of Lambakarna, the Large-Eared Lord, or Lambodara, The Huge-Bellied Lord. Where on earth did they come up with those names?"

I regard the rotund belly and enormous ears, which gently flap. "I can't imagine."

"I am, however, particularly fond of Mahabala, Enormously Strong Lord."

I only needed someone to talk to, and there's nobody else to listen.

"I am listening," Ganesh says.

"You can read my mind?"

"Of course. Your wishes pulled me quite hard. Nearly lost my head again."

"You grant wishes?"

"I destroy obstacles and impediments—"

"You mean you can remove the obstacles in my life?"

"A little more complex than that. Difficult to explain."

"I'm glad you're here, Ganesh, because nothing is going right for me. I want to run away. Cousin Pinky is stealing Jamie. Can you make things right again?"

"Again?" Ganesh raises a golden eyebrow.

"Make Jamie like me, love me."

Ganesh sighs. "If you wish. However, when I remove obstacles, I am removing illusions, helping you see the truth."

"I see the truth! I see Brian calling me a nigger. Mrs. Ghose thinks I'm stupid because I don't speak Bengali. Dad expects me to win the Nobel Prize for physics. We're moving to California, and Jamie thinks he's in love with Pinky. She blinds him with her Kathak dancing. Before she came, he kissed me. There's a big, huge hole in my heart. Jamie is the only boy I've ever loved. I'll love him forever."

Ganesh clears his throat. "I would not be so hasty about forever and all that."

"But it *is* forever. It is, it is!"

Ganesh rolls his eyes. His enormous belly jiggles. "You would like all these obstacles removed, then, is that it?"

"Yes! My parents—I know I should respect them, thank them for everything they've done for me, but I can't help my feelings. Mum won't let me wear lip gloss or sleep over anywhere on a school night or cut and feather my hair. She keeps making rules. Can you—"

"Remove the rules?" Ganesh lets out a deep sigh, blowing a few Jelly Bellies across the floor.

I nod.

"This is why I prefer to avoid the messy business of granting wishes. I don't usually speak to *anyone.*"

"You don't? But aren't you everywhere in India, on T-shirts and handbags, adorning storefronts and homes? That's what Pinky said."

"Of course, but I don't engage in conversation with mortals. However, your keening pierced my rather sensitive ears."

"I was thinking, not keening."

"Your thoughts have a particular high-pitched whine. Difficult to ignore. A bit like a dog whistle."

A dog whistle?

"You've never appeared to Cousin Pinky, then?" I ask.

Ganesh swings his trunk and his nearly human belly moves in and out as he breathes. "She does not perceive her life as problematic. You, on the other hands"—he waves two of his hands—"you see your life as an obstacle course."

"It is. Don't you know . . . I could be Indian for Jamie and for the Ghoses!" My excitement grows. "How I wish to know what they say in Bengali!" I think of the look of pity Mrs. Ghose gave me. "And for Dad to stop picking his nose and telling everyone I'm going to be a physicist—you know? And I don't want to move to California. Can't you make us stay?"

"Are you quite certain?" Ganesh's golden brows furrow.

"Yes, I want to stay near Jamie forever." I'm breathless, greedy. "And I want to be beautiful, with perfect teeth and hair. I want to have a shape, not be skinny and covered in zits forever."

"You will grow and have a shape in good time."

"I don't want to wait!"

"As you like. Your wishes have been granted. The session is now closed."

"Closed? That's it? No waving a wand, abracadabra, back before midnight? I won't turn into a pumpkin?"

"I don't require spells, incantations or props."

"Where will you be?" A sudden pain pierces my heart. "I don't know what I'd do without you to talk to."

"I shall remain for the time being."

MAYA IN WONDERLAND

I wake up to a quiet morning spreading across the sky. Fingers of sunlight reach in through the window.

I sit up and rub my eyes. Did I dream Ganesh? Statues don't grant wishes. There's no such thing as a talking elephant god. He doesn't fit into what Dad taught me about the structure of the universe, Einstein's theory of relativity, the laws of gravity, the cosmos.

I shut my eyes and follow the patterns swirling on the insides of my eyelids. Stars dart away, shifting to blue and red eddies and currents. Ganesh forms a faint golden imprint, a film negative.

My eyes snap open.

Should I go see if he's still in the closet eating Jelly Bellies? I'm afraid to leave the warmth and comfort of my blankets, afraid that he won't be there, that I'll find only a statue and realize I've gone around the bend.

My mouth feels different. I run my tongue along my teeth. No sharp metal. Smooth!

Goose bumps race across my skin.

I jump out of bed and rush to the mirror. My braces have disintegrated. They are no more. My white teeth line up like Chiclets. I close my mouth, smile, open again, smile, run my fingers along my teeth. The braces are really gone. How can they have disappeared overnight?

I touch my cheeks. My skin is warm, resistant to pressure. The floor is cool beneath my bare feet. The world is solid. I pinch my arm, stomp my feet, shake my head. Nothing wakes me.

I study myself in the mirror, and as I watch, my hair grows thicker, shorter and shinier. Cut and feathered! The two zits fade and disappear, leaving no scars.

Underneath striped flannel pajamas, my shape fills out. I slide my hands down along my hips, my thighs. Curves! I blink, shake my head. What's going on? What's happening to me?

This is not my skinny girl-body. This is a woman-body forming in five minutes, mine and not mine. Budding Indian Marilyn Monroe. Slender legs, narrow waist and round boobs. Everything moves from the wrong place to the right place. The cotton pajamas reshape to fit my new figure.

Stardust sprinkles through my brain. I am Maya in Wonderland. If this is a dream, I want to sleep forever.

What else has changed?

I focus on one spot on the wall and whip around in a pirouette. Slide across the floor in a pas de chat. Perfect ballet moves spring from my unconscious mind and shoot lightning messages along my nerves. My limbs react before I can think. The awestruck part of me gazes in astonishment, while the new Maya chassés and pirouettes, shiny hair flying, eyes glinting, smooth skin aglow.

I'm no longer clumsy!

I'm coordinated, not even out of breath. How can this happen?

I fling open the closet. Ganesh's belly rises and falls, ears gently flapping. He is still alive! On hangers above him, new outfits line up in expectation, waiting for me to choose. New jeans, blouses, dresses. Dream clothes.

"Thank you! You're magic!" I pick up Ganesh and kiss his trunk, dance around the room with him.

"Oooohhh," he moans. "Put me down. I feel motion sickness again."

"Sorry—I'm just so happy. You really did grant my wishes!" I put him back in the closet with mounds of candy surrounding him.

He frowns. "In case you have forgotten, I am removing obstacles to finding your truth."

"This *is* my truth!"

In my chest of drawers I discover undershirts and

new bras and bikini cotton underpants printed with the days of the week.

I step back. Hit by a Mack truck. I'm not sure whether to dance or run away. This is what I wanted. I asked for it. Could the rest of the world have adjusted to fit me?

I run to my desk and rummage through the drawers. Pencils, erasers, elastic bands, hastily typewritten stories. Protractor and slide rule and magnifying glass that Dad brought from work to encourage me to become a scientist. Instead, I played Sherlock Holmes. Psycho played Watson.

I search for clues through the lens. My arm appears normal—just the same black hairs and pores. Nothing unusual. I'm not Dorothy viewing the Emerald City through green-tinted spectacles.

I put away the magnifying glass, close the drawers, run to my bed and find my diary in its usual hiding spot under the mattress. My secret codes are still there, my fantasies of the One and yesterday's confessions. My past remains in this dog-eared notebook, and yet my future lies open, its pages blank.

I hear my parents walking around in the master bedroom, Dad humming happily. Pinky's footsteps patter down the hall to her room, then back to the washroom. The door clicks shut. She'll be in there for an hour.

How real this is, how clear the morning, how lucid my mind.

My homework still waits in my knapsack.

Homework!

My hands tremble as I unzip the knapsack and pull out my French notebook. The answers wrote themselves in my handwriting. Without effort, the French words translate into English in my mind.

Quelle idée! What an idea!

Elle devient physicienne. She's becoming a physicist.

Il a les yeux bleus et les cheveux bruns. He has blue eyes and brown hair.

How do I know these phrases? They prance around all by themselves. My insides jump with excitement, and yet a prickling sensation creeps along my skin. Did I write in my sleep? Why don't I remember? This is Ganesh's doing. He granted my wishes.

I put away my homework and peer out the window. The blizzard's aftermath lies before me in layers of white. Snow covers the blueberries, gooseberry bushes and the hedges and grass. Several inches of snow weigh down the weeping willow, the tamarack and silver birch trees.

We're snowed in.

I sit on the bed and rest my head in my hands. My mind spins. I have to walk around in my new body. I wonder what Jamie will think? My friends? The teachers? Mum and Dad?

The smells of frying onion and potato drift into my nose. Mum's cooking on a school day. Usually I'm left to pour my own milk over Froot Loops.

Ganesh sighs from the closet. "Go and have breakfast."

"Don't leave, okay?"

He doesn't reply. His mouth is full of cookies.

I yank on my slippers, race out into the hallway and find Mum in the kitchen. She's not dressed. She's homebody Mum in robe and slippers, humming over a sizzling pan. Exquisite scents rise to my nose. My mouth waters.

"Mum, what are you doing?"

"Making your favorite, darling. Hash browns."

Hash browns! She never calls me darling.

"Thanks, Mum. We don't have school today, do we?" With a certain caution, I step past her and grab my cup of tea. She added just the right amount of milk and sugar. Not too sweet, not too bitter.

"Of course not. The roads are closed."

"You're not going to university?"

"Of course not."

"And Dad?"

"He's not going to work either. He may go cross-country skiing."

Cross-country skiing? No lectures?

I give Mum a wide, toothy grin. "Look, no braces!"

She glances up. "Why, of course you have no braces, darling. Would you like some?" Her eyes are darker than usual.

"No, I never want braces," I say.

"Then you shall never have them."

"Look at my pirouette." I whirl around in my pajamas. "Perfect!"

"Do I look older to you? Different?"

She gives me the once-over. "No difference. Beautiful as always."

I step closer. She doesn't notice my curves or boobs or shiny hair or smooth skin. She doesn't know. It's like the old Maya never existed.

I wonder whether my friends will see the change.

"Can Psycho and Sally come over?"

"Of course. Anything you want."

"Anything? Can Dad make a fire?"

Mum nods, humming a melodic Hindi tune under her breath.

I like this Mum, the one who stays home to make breakfast, who doesn't leave me at the mercy of Dad's supper experiments. This Mum lets my friends come over, calls me darling and tells me I can have anything I want.

Possibilities swoop in faster than the speed of light. Mum might let me wear lip gloss, finally.

I slip back into my room with a plate of chocolate chip cookies for Ganesh.

"Have you got more of the Licorice Jelly Bellies?" he asks, biting into a cookie. Crumbs fall on his golden feet.

"Don't you ever stop eating?" I can't stop staring at this living elephant, his trunk swishing.

"I love the Jelly Bellies!"

"Try eating fruits and vegetables. Grains or protein. Meat and poultry. From the four food groups."

Ganesh waves an arm. "Food groups, schmood groups. Hang around twenty years and the whole concept of nutrition will radically change. Not as much meat recommended, for one thing—"

"You know the future?"

Ganesh nods, ears flapping.

If he knows the future, I could ask what I'll be when I grow up, whether Jamie and I will have children, when I will die and when my parents will die.

"Yes, you could ask," Ganesh says.

I hold up my hand, panic inside me. "I was just thinking. I don't really want to know."

"You made your wishes."

"I'm growing up so fast!"

"You didn't wish to change slowly." He talks with his mouth full, chocolate smeared on his lips.

"Can you slow it down?"

"I specialize in granting boons, not slowing things down. Now go and enjoy what you wished for."

SNOW DAY

SALLY and Psycho show up after breakfast.

"Notice anything different about me?" I ask as they stomp snow from their boots and peel off their parkas in the foyer. Pinky stands behind me in silence. She has lost her starlight glow of charisma. Nobody notices. Not even her. She seems to think she has always been shy.

"Is this a game? Charades?" Psycho peers at me.

"You brushed your teeth for once?" Sally laughs as if she just made a big joke.

Mum hums in the kitchen in oblivion.

"My braces are gone." I bare my teeth. "What do you think?"

No oohs or aahs or gasps of surprise.

"You had braces?" Sally asks.

"You're getting them?" Psycho exclaims. "Why? Your teeth are so straight. You are so lucky!"

"I wish I had your smile," Pinky says.

"I'm not getting braces! I had them, remember?" I frown.

My friends stare blankly at me, then at each other.

"You know—zits, braces. Ponytails." I flip my feathered hair.

Psycho narrows her gaze at me. "You want ponytails?"

"I don't want them. I used to have them."

"When you were about three years old, maybe." Sally snickers.

"You don't remember . . ." My voice trails away. I think of Mum, who didn't notice any change in me, either.

"You are so perfect," Sally says. She doesn't turn up her nose. She stares the way she stared at Jamie that day during lunch, when he ate my samosas.

"I'm not perfect!" Just prettier, stronger and more coordinated than I was. I demonstrate my pirouette and pas de chat down the hall.

My friends and Pinky watch in awe.

"You are so good." Psycho claps. "Show me how to do that."

"Yeah, me too. I wish I could do that," Sally says.

"So do I," Pinky says.

Nobody remembers the old Maya. I consider showing them my diary. Not yet. My secret thoughts are private, between Anne Frank and me.

I follow my friends and Pinky down to the basement, where we play tennis against the concrete wall until Mum calls us for lunch.

She makes peanut butter sandwiches, mayonnaise-and-chip sandwiches for Sally.

"Wow, your mom is great," Sally says.

I ask to sleep over at Sally's, and Mum and Mrs. Weston both say yes. On a weeknight! I can hardly wait.

After lunch, we go tobogganing on the Kinsey House field. The sun is out, our street newly cleared. By Ganesh's magic, the snowplow broke down right at the school entrance.

We glide down the hills on our toboggans and plastic Krazy Karpets. Each run is perfect and fast, snow spraying our faces, our laughter echoing off the hotel wall.

Dad cross-country skis onto the field and waves as he passes. We all wave back. I'm glad Dad is not lecturing at the plant, in Amsterdam or in Palo Alto. He's home, near us, and he's enjoying my wishes too.

"Your dad is groovy," Psycho says as she pushes off and flies down the hill. I flop onto my Krazy Karpet and follow. We careen down the snowy hillside, faster and faster until the cold air sucks our breath away.

At the bottom, we slide through the dip and up the other side, then back down. Pinky oozes down the hill on Mum's heavy toboggan and soon comes to a slow, unceremonious stop.

Then I see him.

Jamie lopes down Massey Road, a big snow shovel tucked under his arm. I turn away, pretending not to notice, but my insides dance with anticipation.

He strides to the hilltop. I hold my breath. Will he remember the old Maya?

Pinky reaches the bottom of the hill on the slow toboggan.

"Let's see what this baby can do." Jamie sits on the shovel, grabs the handle and shoves off. Whooping all the way down, he slides farther than anyone else.

"Look at him go!" Sally clambers back up the hill.

"That's Jamie Klassen?" Psycho opens her mouth in awe. "Riding a shovel? *The* Jamie Klassen?"

"That's his name, don't wear it out." I watch Jamie clamber up the hill. In his hands, the shovel is cool, the latest fad.

Psycho and Sally sit on Sally's Krazy Karpet, push off and fly down at an angle, leaning sideways, and what happens next seems to occur in slow motion. Bright rays of sun reflect off the white field in a million shards of light. Psycho and Sally rush down and down and then, boom, they crash into Pinky. She flies backward through the air and lands on Psycho. The Krazy Karpet springs from Psycho's hands and slides down as if ridden by a ghost.

Jamie and I race down the hill. Psycho and Sally are okay. Pinky sits with her hands covering her face.

"Oh, Shiva!" She rocks back and forth, her mittens over her nose.

"Let me see." I yank her hands away from her face. A cut on her nose oozes bright red blood.

"M-my nose!" she sputters.

My stomach twists into a knot of guilt. Maybe this accident had nothing to do with my wishes, but I'm not so sure.

HUMPTY DUMPTY

THIS is my first time sleeping over at Sally's house.

Mrs. Weston has her hair pulled back in a tight bun, as if having hair irritates her. Her ears and cheeks look pulled back too. Her face must *hurt*.

Her white peasant shirt ruffles in the front, and her stockings are tight and sheer. Who wears stockings at home?

"Just let me take that." She grabs my bag, as if it is already messing up the house. She's as picky neat as Mum, only Mum has changed.

I glance left into the kitchen. The countertop shines. No plates, morning teacups or crumbs. Maybe the Westons don't eat.

My stomach growls as Mrs. Weston leads me down a carpeted hallway to Sally's room, which overflows with frills. Sally is sitting cross-legged on an enormous bed with brass bedposts.

Bedknobs and broomsticks.

She's dressing Barbie dolls in miniature ski suits. She yanks a grape Tootsie pop from her mouth and shoves it under her pillow, where it's sure to stick to the sheets.

"Haven't I told you time and time again, no eating between meals?" Mrs. Weston says.

"I'm not eating. When's supper?" Sally grins, a purple stain on her tongue.

"When your father gets home."

Mum never calls Dad "your father." Panic rises in my chest. I'm starving. My stomach protests, but I dare not ask for even a cracker. How can a home be filled with furniture and yet not have food? My parents don't have much furniture, but we always have food.

I'll have to jump out the window and eat snow, or maybe run home. My parents never forbid me to eat when I'm hungry.

Mrs. Weston shuffles away down the hall.

I look around for books, but Sally doesn't have even a magazine. She used to have *Road & Track* when her brother lived at home. Now he drives a tractor on a farm near Lac du Bonnet.

She owns a hundred blankets, flouncy dresses and dolls, but nothing to read, so I settle for playing Monopoly with her on the bed.

Sally steals two $500 bills from the bank, but who cares anyway because she lands on the hotels I bought for Boardwalk and Park Place, and she goes broke.

If only I could change into my pajamas. Mrs. Weston wouldn't approve. She wears special indoor shoes that look like hospital slippers. Skirt and peasant blouse and sheer stockings. She walks stiffly, tightly, as though she's going to work, except she's only going to the living room.

Odors of meat and eggs waft in. The smell makes me gag, hungry as I am. We stopped eating meat when vegetarian Pinky arrived.

In a strange way, I miss her right now.

A bell rings in the kitchen.

"Supper!" Sally leaps off the bed as if she hasn't eaten in a year. We are cows charging to the dining room for our hay.

At the table, I'm afraid to touch the silver knives and forks and delicate china hand-painted in blue floral patterns. Mrs. Weston has laid the table for a formal feast. No wonder Sally eats so sloppily at school, the only place she can relax.

I sit with my hands clasped in my lap, my knuckles turning white. At home, we use the good silver and china only for special guests, usually Dad's colleagues from the plant. Indian friends eat with their hands, the way Sahadev and Vishnu ate at the Ghoses.

I know I wanted to sleep over at a friend's house on a school night, but what if I drop a plate? Mrs. Weston will swoop down upon me in all her wrath.

Mr. Weston saunters in from the living room with a newspaper tucked under his arm. He's tall, dark and long in body, nose and limb, the opposite of Sally's mom. Abbott and Costello, I am thinking. Sylvester and Tweety.

Mrs. Weston brings a tray of glass goblets filled with milk, then eggs in silver cups.

Eggs, for supper?

Sally knows I hate eggs! Everyone knows.

I could try to eat the egg while holding my breath. Just swallow. Perhaps I could accidentally drop the egg. Humpty Dumpty was an egg, after all, and he took a great fall.

I could say I'm allergic, though I'm actually allergic only to Chinese mushrooms, the black kind Dad mixes into his international concoctions, if he still makes them in my wished-for world.

The Westons bow their heads and hold hands around the table. We don't do this during supper at home, this séance thing, but I go along for the ride. Through certain moments, like saying grace or the Lord's Prayer and singing "O Canada," I know to go along.

"Thank you, Lord, for blessing us with time to make supper," Mrs. Weston says in an irritated voice. "Thank you for giving us food for our plates."

Against unspoken rules, I keep an eye open on Mr.

Weston, who droops in his chair across the table. He keeps one eye open too, on the business page of the *Winnipeg Free Press*. He notices me looking and winks. I focus on my plate and try not to smile.

Mrs. Weston thanks God and then says, "Please make us worthy." I think of the Lord's Prayer, which we recite every morning at school, and "Give us this day our daily bread," and I wonder whether the Westons have their daily bread every night with eggs.

"Amen," the family choruses; then they let go of each other's hands and whack their spoons against their eggshells. I watch and do the same. The top of the shell implodes, but there is still an unbroken membrane underneath. Beneath the film, soft, yellow liquid slides around as if alive.

The egg taunts me with its sulfur stink. My throat closes up. Mr. Weston slices the top off his egg, tilts his head back and tips the bottom into his mouth. As he slurps, the yolk trickles down his beard. He picks up the napkin and wipes his chin.

Stifling a gag, I sink the spoon into the yolk and dither, buying time.

Mrs. Weston slices her egg through the middle. The top half of the shell lies dead on the plate as she spoons the egg into her mouth and swallows. Horror. I picture the yolk slithering down her throat.

I lift the spoon to my mouth. The egg sloshes around. I can't wish for this supper to disappear.

"It's raw," I say.

"I beg your pardon?" Mrs. Weston looks up from her plate.

"I eat only hard-boiled eggs, and only sometimes." I want to say I don't like eggs, but that would be even ruder.

"My word." Mrs. Weston pushes her chair back, gets up and snatches my eggcup.

Thank you, Ganesh, I am thinking.

"I'll make you another one. Hard-boiled." Mrs. Weston goes to the kitchen.

Another one?

Mrs. Weston brings a new egg, still too runny, then another and another. An endless army of soft-boiled eggs march across my plate; then the telephone rings and Mrs. Weston runs to the hall to answer.

One last chance. I glance sidelong at Sally, who is lost in her meat loaf, then lift the egg from the cup and look at Mr. Weston. He looks at me. We trade glances across the table.

Mrs. Weston talks softly in the hall. I hold out the egg to Mr. Weston. He doesn't take it. If Dad were here, he would grab the egg and pop it into his mouth.

How I miss my dad, only I don't know if my new dad, the one I wished for, will steal food from my plate. An urge comes to me to run home and find out.

I have no choice but to pop the egg into my mouth, chew fast and swallow as Mrs. Weston walks back in. I concentrate on ignoring the squishy egg taste. It's all I can do not to vomit.

"I'm not feeling well," I say. "I might've caught a virus. Thank you very much for supper. I have to go home."

CLOSER

AT home, supper is almost ready. I don't have to lay the table, place the knives and forks and place mats in the proper symmetry. Mum doesn't scold me for trailing snow through the hall. She doesn't ask why I came back early or tell me to clean up and wash my hands.

Pencils, paper, books and Kleenex are strewn in a mess in my room. Mum didn't pick up my socks. She doesn't come in and tell me it looks as though a hurricane struck.

Supper consists of my favorite foods. Wonton soup,

Shirley Temples with three maraschino cherries, Brussels sprouts, enormous French fries, and sliced cantaloupe for dessert, even though cantaloupe doesn't grow in winter.

Ganesh makes anything possible.

Dad eats without glancing at my plate, and Pinky sulks, only a trace of brightness in her eyes. She plays with her food, pushes the melon around on her plate.

I did not consider that she might not like cantaloupe. I feel a pang of pity. I hold out my plate and use my best whining voice. "You got more than I did! I want some of yours."

Pinky lets out a perceptible sigh of relief and wastes no time scooping the cantaloupe onto my plate.

Mum doesn't scold me. A strange look comes into her eyes. She drifts away and leaves behind a mannequin. Then, just as quickly, awareness slips back into her eyes. She smiles and shovels Brussels sprouts into her mouth.

Dad keeps eating without stealing food, and after supper, he makes a fire in the family room fireplace.

Mum empties a bag of marshmallows into a bowl. She knows I love to roast marshmallows. Maybe this will cheer up Pinky, too.

Then the telephone on the kitchen wall rings.

"For you, Maya darling." Mum holds out the receiver.

My heart tap-taps. "Who is it?"

"Some boy." Mum's voice is wrong, lopsided, like a falling cake.

Some boy and she isn't angry? No questions? No lecture about rules? I rush over and grab the receiver. "This is Maya."

"I need to talk to you. I have to see you."

My heart skips. I know this deep voice.

"Something is happening," Jamie whispers.

"What? Are you sick? Is your house on fire?"

"I don't think so. I didn't see flames."

I suck in a breath. "Then what is it?"

Pinky slinks by, pours herself a glass of water and goes back to the family room.

I imagine Ganesh chomping in the closet, laughing to himself. By tomorrow, he may run out of sweets.

"I'm not sure why I called." Jamie's voice goes hard.

"Are you okay? You sound different."

Jamie sighs, and his tone softens. "It's like someone reached into my head and turned my brain around."

"Does it hurt?"

"Kind of tingles."

I wait, listening to the stove clock tick, tick, tick. Pinky, Mum and Dad laugh by the crackling fire.

"I'm losing my mind," Jamie says finally. He hangs up, and I'm left with a dial tone.

I grab a handful of marshmallows on my way to my bedroom.

"Jamie is supposed to love me!" I whisper to Ganesh.

"Ah, new sweets! What is this?" Ganesh's golden

trunk unfurls, wraps around a marshmallow and stuffs it into his mouth.

"You didn't answer my question."

"Perhaps he does not yet know what he feels." Ganesh lifts an eyebrow. "Mortals need time to understand the truth."

MAGICAL MYSTERY TOUR

THIS is how the next day goes.

I drink perfect tea and a homemade breakfast, and Dad leaves for work whistling disco instead of oldies. He promises to pick up my favorite supper on the way home. Mum cooks and hums and cleans, and doesn't tell me to tidy my room or do my homework.

Pinky walks to school with me in silence, her nose puffy from her tobogganing accident. She hides her face in her desk until Miss Barth gives her detention.

I do perfectly in French. Miss Barth smiles until her

skin nearly cracks, and praises me for living up to my True Potential. I should be happy.

At lunch, Jamie sits close, looking a bit stunned, as if he doesn't yet know why he wants to be next to me.

Brian has laryngitis. He doesn't come to school. Pinky doesn't make it to the cafeteria for lunch. She banged her nose on the desk and opened the wound again.

I'm not feeling so hot about any of this.

Jamie sticks to me at recess, his mouth open in surprise, as though he has just seen the answer to a complicated algebra question.

I wait with infinite patience. I have the rest of my life.

In ballet, I practice my perfect pirouettes and soon all the kids gather around to watch the girl who once wiped out on her tailbone.

I bet they don't even remember. Miss Barth doesn't yell my name, "Mayo-Scary." She's in awe of me, and Kathy Linton asks if she can be my best friend, and then all the kids want to be my best friend, just like that.

After school, Jamie and I go Krazy Karpeting together with Psycho and Sally, and then Jamie and I gallivant all over town, throwing snowballs at each other, laughing and hurling each other into snowbanks.

When I get home, just like magic, a real mailbox stands at the end of our driveway. The metal gleams in yellow, with painted green vines and white crocuses. Presto, all the houses have mailboxes now, and a real mailman drives down the road in a white truck that looks like the summertime ice cream truck.

I watch him wave as he shoves envelopes into each box.

I pick up the bills—no letter from a boyfriend yet, but I hope one is coming.

I'm on a Ganesh Magical Mystery Tour. I'm giddy, overflowing with possibility, waiting for Jamie to realize why he wants to be with me all the time, while Pinky sits in detention with her head stuck in the desk. Serves her right, I'm thinking, but a queasiness comes over me.

Must be the memory of eggs at Sally Weston's house. I forgot to wish all the eggs away into the Twilight Zone.

BUTTERFLY WINGS

MORNING opens like a tulip sprinkling pink petals across the sky. In the kitchen, Mum makes toast. Her eyes are a shade darker than they were yesterday. Pathways into the unknown. Her skin is a shade paler, or maybe it's the winter light.

I step back. My frightened self wants to run and hide, but the fascinated part keeps me watching.

"What would you like for lunch?" she asks.

I glance past her at the countertop. "Peanut butter sandwich?"

"Whatever you like."

"What if I want cheese?" I sidle by and grab my teacup, sip flawless First Flush, sweet and smooth, better than yesterday's tea.

She opens the fridge. "We have cheese—"

"Tomatoes and celery?" I dip into black waters, testing for possibilities, for monsters.

She closes the fridge. "We have tomatoes and celery."

"Chicken salad?"

"If you like."

"The peanut butter is fine, just fine."

She nods, then shakes her head briskly, as if to dislodge a stuck thought, then smiles. A smile filled with nothing. "Can I make hash browns, darling? Adjust the thermostat? Are you cold?"

"I'm fine." Has her skin grown even paler in the past five minutes? Did I wish for this?

"Drink for lunch? Fanta?" she asks, then glances at her watch.

"Isn't that bad for my teeth?"

She nods, looking confused, and hurries into the hall.

She looks exactly like my mother, has the same voice, but she's not my mother. Then who is she?

In my bedroom closet, I touch the top of Ganesh's elephant head. His eyes are closed, his belly gently rising and falling.

"Wake up!" I whisper. "What did you do to my mother?"

His eyes flutter open. "I have done nothing to her."

"But she says 'Whatever you like' to everything!"

"Indeed."

"Indeed? Is that all you can say?" I should be ecstatic, so why does fear tug me into its undertow?

I'm getting dressed when I hear a splat against my bedroom window. I lean over and press my nose to the glass. Snow slides down. A snowball thrown against the house? I cup my hands on the window so I can see out. Jamie waves from the yard.

I slide open the window, and cold air rushes in through the screen.

"What are you doing here?" I whisper, too loud.

If anyone could see, my smile would take up my whole face.

Jamie trudges closer. He's so handsome in his bomber jacket, right below my window.

I'm eager to run outside.

"Rapunzel, Rapunzel, let down your hair," he jokes; then his eyes open in surprise, as if the words popped out all by themselves.

"You'll catch pneumonia standing out there!"

Jamie looks up at me and blinks. "I dreamed about you last night. It's all hazy now." He rubs his forehead.

Footsteps in the hall again.

"You'd better go," I say. "Someone's coming."

I shut the window and slide the curtains across just as Mum wanders in.

"Oh. I thought I heard voices." Blank smile.

"I was praying . . . to Ganesh."

Mum looks around.

"He's in the closet," I say. "For privacy."

"Let's get some daylight in here." She yanks open the curtains.

This is it. I'm dead.

She stands there, gazing out as the seconds tick by.

I dare not speak. Ganesh, help me now. I'll have to make up a story to explain Jamie standing in the snow beneath my window.

The seconds turn into a minute.

"I've been thinking about the future." Mum turns toward me. Her eyes are still dim.

Jamie must've left.

I sit on the bed and let out a long breath. I won't look directly into her eyes. Then everything will be okay.

She tilts her head, as if there's water in her ear.

"What's wrong with you, Mum?"

"It's as though someone reached into my skull and—"

"Turned your brain around?"

She nods. "How did you know?"

"Lucky guess." I'm going to throw up.

"Well." She sighs. "Dad and I thought it would be best if we stay here. You wouldn't have to leave your friends. You could finish school in a familiar place. It's important for a child to have stability." She is talking to herself, or maybe someone else is talking through her.

"Are you sure? What about your teaching job in California? Shouldn't we go where the opportunities are?"

Mum looks startled. "Is that what you want? To move?"

"No. I mean yes. I don't know!"

"Let me know when you make up your mind."

As she gets up, I catch a glimpse of my real mother. I'm sure it is her, a flash of bright butterfly wings in a dark wood. Then she is gone.

DREAMWORLD

DAD kisses my cheek. "Have a good day. I'll miss you. Can't wait to get home." He blinks blank eyes and leaves a cloud of Brut aftershave behind.

With the grown-ups gone, I tiptoe into their room to steal extra nickels and dimes to buy sweets for Ganesh. I wonder if Dad thinks his coins disappear into Night-stand Land, the way socks disappear into Dryer Land. I keep a log in my diary of coins borrowed. They go to a good cause, to keep Ganesh happy.

Something is terribly wrong with Dad's nightstand.

The bills are separated into neat piles in the drawer.

His books are lined up according to height. When I slide the drawer open and shut, nothing falls out.

He has arranged the coins in neat little towers. Dimes, nickels, quarters and pennies. My fingers itch to mix up the pile, mess up everything.

I want the Dad whose mind reaches out to the speed of light. I want my hip version of Einstein back, the one who picks his nose.

Perfect Dad doesn't pick his nose or conduct supper experiments. This should feel good, right? Victory. Only I have an about-to-vomit kind of feeling. Saliva on my tongue.

My old Dad is gone. I knew this today, when I saw his fathomless, nothing eyes.

I toss the dimes in my hand. These coins are thin, yet dimes are worth twice as much as heavier nickels, maybe because of the imprint of the schooner *Bluenose*, the pride of Canadian yachting. After the *Bluenose* ran aground, a replica, *Bluenose II*, was built as a touring ship. I realize that this is what has happened. My parents have run aground, and I'm living with replicas.

❋ ❋ ❋

Jamie is standing in our driveway.

My heart stops, then starts up again. Do I look sleepy? Is my hair a mess?

I step out into the cold. Pinky bumps into my back and says, *"Dekho!"* and this time I understand. Neon letters form refrigerator-magnet English words in my head.

"Why don't *you* watch out?" I stomp down the porch steps.

"You stopped right in front of me!" She shoves by me, glides toward Jamie and bats her eyelashes.

Jamie stares at her, a flicker of confusion in his eyes. I must be patient. He doesn't yet know that he loves me.

I open and close the bright mailbox a few times before leaving. I love the metallic squeak of the hinges, the smell of new paint.

All the way to school, Pinky chatters at Jamie, but her words leave a forgotten trail in the snow. She sulks away, head down, and spends most of the day in the nurse's office or the washroom.

The morning passes in an inside-out, backward dreamworld. Ms. Redburn is the same and notices no change in me. She doesn't know I turned everything backward and inside out. She doesn't know I haven't always been beautiful.

Miss Barth no longer stinks of rubbing alcohol but carries the faint scent of cinnamon cookies.

At lunch in the cafeteria, there's no sign of Pinky or Brian. I breeze through the afternoon, wait for Jamie to come around, but always I think of my parents' blank eyes and *Whatever you want, Maya. Let me know when you make up your mind.*

After school, I step outside and there he is, waiting near the monkey bars, holding up a cutout heart painted in big black letters, MAYA 4-EVER.

MAYA AND THE WOLF

MY face turns beet red. I can feel the heat.

Two of Jamie's classmates saunter by, glancing at the card in his hand. He gazes at me through hypnotized eyes.

My mouth goes dry. Kids rush and tumble out around me. Their laughter barely registers in my mind as I watch Jamie walk, or rather stumble, toward me.

My insides flutter as he draws near. Seeing him brings a painful squeeze to my rib cage.

He crosses the sidewalk and stops two steps away. Our gazes collide, bam. In a flash, the kiss comes back vividly.

Yes, there is a reason for this magic. He's so good-looking, the kind of handsome that pierces my heart. All he has to do is stand there. Maybe I can teach him not to overdo it.

"I'll do anything," he whispers close to my face. His breath blows ripples of warmth across my skin.

"Anything what?" I have no idea what he means, or maybe I do and want to pretend I don't.

"I could serenade you—"

"No—"

Already he is singing softly.

I did not know this before: one thing Jamie can't do is sing. He wanders off-key along a precarious ledge.

"Stop, enough!" I yank him back from the brink.

"Your wish is my command."

Isn't that the truth.

His in-love eyes clear. He blinks, dazed, as if he just woke up.

"What the—" He glances at me, shakes his head. "What is this? What am I doing?"

"The card, in your hand," I say.

Kids glance over and whisper as they pass.

"I made this for you," he says.

"Please—" I wince. But the old Jamie wanted Pinky. The new Jamie will have to do.

I open the card:

Roses are red,
Violets are blue.

One thing is true—
I do love you.

Not the most original poem I've ever read. It's the thought that counts, and the word *love* blazes inside me.

"This is so sweet, Jamie," I say, "but it's not Valentine's Day."

His eyes widen; he steps back and a blast of wind ruffles his hair. The lightbulb epiphany glows above his head.

"That's it," he whispers. "The reason my brain is on backward."

"Jamie, I—"

"I love you."

I turn on my heel and start for home. "Why the sudden change of heart?"

"I—I don't know. There is no why. I just love you."

"Yes, but what do you love about me?"

"When I think of Maya, I think . . . I love her. I want to be with her all the time."

"Why, Jamie?"

"Because you're beautiful and perfect."

"But what about before?"

"Before?"

"Never mind." For Jamie, for everyone but me, there is no before. There is only now. Maybe Jamie loves me because I don't have braces. My hair shines, and I probably won't need Clearasil as long as I live.

He loves me for who he thinks I am.

"What about Pinky?" I ask.

"Who?"

I'm about to say, *You know, my cousin, the most ravishing, exotic Indian Kathak dancer on earth? The one with boobs?* Jamie won't remember.

"Will you marry me?" he asks.

"What? I'm too young to get engaged—"

Whoa. Mum is supposed to say this, not me.

"You are never too young," Jamie says as we pass a gaggle of kids at the corner. They watch us sidelong.

"Look, I have homework." I hurry up the hill. "I'm going home. I'm not thinking about—"

"I'll go too." He walks so close, his bomber jacket swishes against my parka.

"I have to buy some candy at the drugstore first."

Now that we have a bright, groovy mailbox at the end of our driveway, I no longer have to pick up the mail at the post office. What will I do with the new hole in the afternoon?

Pinky walked home with Psycho and Sally. Did they go to Psycho's house to watch TV without me? To play Ouija? Or to do homework together, to the library? What are they talking about? Is Pinky crying?

A rock of guilt rolls through me. My wishes came out twisted, the way they did in "The Monkey's Paw," when the man wished his son back from the grave and then had to wish him away.

I can't wish Jamie away.

In the drugstore, he stands right next to me and sniffs my hair. "You smell good."

"My natural smell," I lie. It's Chantilly.

Jamie helps me choose candy for Ganesh, which requires three weeks of allowance and all the coins I stole.

At home, the windows are dark. Jamie follows me up onto the porch. I have an unreasonable urge to swat him away. Only I must remember, I'm in love with him. We're going to get married, have children and live happily ever after. But not today.

"Let me come in," he says.

Or I'll huff, and I'll puff, and I'll blow your house down.

"Won't your dad wonder where you are?"

"I don't care," he says. "I want to stay with you. Can I sleep in your bed, or even under your bed? Or in your closet. Let me look at you all day and night."

I have to talk to Ganesh.

"My eyes get puffy when I sleep," I say. "My hair sticks out."

"I don't care." He shoves the door open, takes off his boots and follows me to my room. My insides are more at war than they were before. Before my wishes, I wanted Jamie.

Today, I still want him. The flutters go through me. There's another part of me squished and suffocated. Still, I let him come into our house.

I call out for Mum and Dad and Pinky, but the rooms are empty in a new, frightening way.

"Where is everyone?" Jamie sounds thrilled that he has me to himself.

"I don't know, but I'm about to find out." As soon as I shower Ganesh with S-W-E-E-T-S, the world will right itself, tilt back into its proper orbit. Everything will return to normal. Go straight to Ganesh, Do Not Pass Go, Do Not Collect $200.

When we get to the closet, Ganesh is gone.

WHAT MAYA WANTS

"WHAT would you like for lunch?" Mum asks as she makes my morning tea.

"Fried rubber boots," I say, knowing Jamie is probably already standing outside my bedroom window. I refuse to look.

"Which boots, dear?" Mum's black eyes don't blink.

"I don't really want fried rubber boots for lunch!"

"Let me know when you make up your mind."

"Slow-cooked birch bark."

"Marinated, darling?"

I understand everything Mum and Dad say in Bengali

now, only who cares because they don't say anything controversial, not anymore. They talk about what Maya wants, what Maya needs, what would make Maya happiest. Only if Maya agrees.

The vacancy inside me grows colder and darker, becomes a mansion of interconnected rooms, all empty and wanting.

I have to find Ganesh.

The problem is, Pinky packed him along with her kohl, Maybelline lipsticks, saris and bangles and returned to India.

"Mum, why did Pinky leave so quickly?" I ask casually.

"Her uncle took ill." Mum pours another cup of tea. Her fingers tremble slightly. "Dad drove her to the airport. She caught a flight to Calcutta. She told me to give you hugs and kisses and say good-bye."

"Why didn't anyone tell me she was leaving? Why didn't she say good-bye to me herself?"

Mum frowns at the calendar tacked to the kitchen wall. "They didn't have time to go back to the school and find you, Maya. She thought you'd understand. The flight left at—"

"She didn't have any fun here, did she? It was 'too bloody cold,' and she cut her nose tobogganing. That's why she left so soon, isn't it?" She liked Jamie, but he didn't notice her in my wished-for world.

Mum tears her gaze from the calendar and wipes the countertop. "Maya, this has nothing to do with you. It was a family emergency."

I know what kind of emergency it was. Pinky would rather be in India or London, anywhere but here. How can I blame her?

She took Ganesh because he belongs to her. He has always been in our family.

Maybe he will return for the Jelly Bellies. If I had rushed home sooner, perhaps brought the candy at lunchtime, would Ganesh have stayed? Did he leave because I starved him?

I had to go to school, I think. I hope Ganesh can hear my thoughts as he bounces around in Pinky's suitcase. He probably has motion sickness.

I should have fed him every half hour, prayed to him, thanked him. I should have showered him with candy.

It is a long way to India—fifty or sixty million miles, give or take. Maybe Pinky's plane hasn't yet touched down in Calcutta. I could wish her back, will her to return.

She doesn't come back.

✳ ✳ ✳

Jamie walks me to school. He sticks to me at lunch, walks me home. My friends can't get close to me. Jamie's friends abandon him and he doesn't care. His grades slip. I wake up in the night and he is there, watching through the window. A hairy feeling creeps along my flesh when I imagine him awake all night with those thirsty eyes.

He calls at all hours and wants to do his homework with me every day. My parents' eyes show blank approval.

I don't have to give piano lessons to the Ghose boys, and I don't have to endure supper at their house.

I lie in bed as a new sense of knowing clears a bigger space of loneliness inside me. It's like waking up from a nap and realizing the sun is already setting and you've missed the whole day. You're wide awake while everyone else is going to bed. You sprinkled sleeping dust in their eyes. They will never wake up, and I will never leave this town.

This was my wish, to grow up here. I'll learn to drive, decide whom to date, what college to attend and what to do for a living, all without my parents' advice. Mum and Dad will say *Whatever Maya wants, Whatever Maya needs* for the rest of their lives. They will never know what they want for themselves or for me.

What happens if I move out of the house? Will my wishes allow me to leave? Will my parents remember to make supper for themselves? Pay the bills, go to work, visit their friends? Or will they wait for me to call and tell them what I want?

My chest aches with sadness. Then I remember what Ganesh said when he granted my wishes.

I am available in clay, carved wood or brass, reading or reclining, seated or dancing, surrounded by skulls.

I sit up. Maybe there is hope.

BACKUP PLAN

THE Ghoses went to Winnipeg and may return home
tomorrow.

I can't reach their statue of Ganesh in the bedroom,
and there's no telling what will happen if I wait too long.
Mum and Dad could turn into transparent ghosts. The
thought gives me chills.

"Can we go and find the Ghoses?" I ask Mum.

"I'll drive you to Winnipeg and we'll search." She
grabs the car keys.

"Mum, do you have a name, an address? A number?
A hint?"

She shakes her head. "We'll search every house until we find them."

"No! I don't want that." I wave my hands through the air. "Forget it, Mum. I don't need to see them."

"Are you sure?"

I nod. I consider asking Mum to help me break into the Ghoses' house while they're gone, but I can't bring myself to give her a criminal record or turn myself into an outlaw just yet.

Maybe tomorrow.

I put the backup plan into action. First I have to get Jamie out of my hair.

After school, I fake being sick. I pretend to heave.

"I'll clean up after you," he coos in my ear.

Even vomit will not drive him away. I manage to shove him down the steps and send him home, for now.

I rush to the phone and call Psycho. Unlike Sally, Psycho can keep a secret, and right now I need a friend. I explain as much as she needs to know.

She's not a skeptic. After all, she believes in *The Exorcist*, the shark from *Jaws* and the aliens in *Invasion of the Body Snatchers*.

"I need to switch parkas with you," I say. "Just for a while."

Oh, Ganesh, I pray, let me make it to the library without Jamie stepping on my heels.

The backup plan rolls. Psycho walks by my house. Hunched over, hood up, she is me in my parka, give or take a few pounds. Jamie follows. She speeds up, he speeds up.

I go to my room and slip on Psycho's parka, boots and scarf. I bundle up and head for the back door, past Mum in the kitchen.

"Oh—I thought you were Celia McCann," she says.

"I stole her parka," I say.

"You must need it. Shall we buy you a new one? Has your old one gone out of fashion?"

"No, it hasn't! My parka is in perfect condition."

Mum stops stirring for a moment and stares at me with her Twilight Zone eyes.

I don't have much time.

"I'm going out," I say, and Mum nods. She's thinner today, more insubstantial. I can see the outline of the countertop through her.

Oh, what have I done?

I force my feet to move out the back door, trudge through the snow. I cut across the backyard and trespass through the neighbors' yard. No sign of Jamie or Psycho. I glance over my shoulder, watch for Jamie's encroaching shadow.

When I reach the library, Psycho is there, puffing, her face red with a sheen of sweat. My open parka hangs crookedly from her shoulders. Her orange hair sticks out everywhere. She staggers forward and grabs my shoulders.

"He chased me!" she pants. "He thought I was you. Good thing I can run faster than him."

This surprises me. "Are you sure?"

"For now. Hurry." She glances left and right, and then her mouth freezes in an O of shock.

I slowly turn, and there is Jamie. If he gets too close, I might lose my nerve.

"What's going on?" He throws Psycho the evil eye, then gives me the love look. "Why are you wearing each other's parkas?"

"We, uh, wanted to switch," I say.

"Yeah. It's a game," Psycho says.

Jamie's eyelids narrow to slits. "You weren't trying to trick me?"

"No! I love Maya's parka." Psycho smooths the sleeves.

"And I love Psycho's." If I were Pinocchio, my nose would grow all the way to Winnipeg.

"I almost thought you were running away, Maya. If you were, I don't know what I'd do." Desperation slices through Jamie's voice.

My heart races as I digest what he just said. Psycho stares at me, wide-eyed.

"What would you do, Jamie?" I ask.

"If you were in disguise, and tried to escape me, well then, I would have to find you." His voice is soft, ominous.

"What if I went really far away?"

"Then I'd follow. I can't live without you. You know that."

"Of course. You won't ever have to live without me."

Psycho and I trade glances.

"Good." Jamie blows steam rings into the air. "Are we going into the library?"

I nod and focus on what Dad told me. I have always been stubborn, and now I must also be brave. I must complete the next phase of the backup plan.

Psycho steps aside as Jamie and I enter, his long legs in easy stride beside me.

He will not derail my plan.

There aren't many people here today. The library is a warm world all its own.

Miss Opie, the librarian, looks up from the reshelving cart.

"Well, hello, Maya," she says, book in hand. "Jamie." She says his name with no surprise, as if he comes in here all the time. She's young, as young as Mum, and slim, with long blond hair and a kind face.

I go to the catalog and pull out the *E* drawer. *Elephant. Elephants. Elephants—Botswana; Elephants—folklore; Elephants—fossil.* Jamie's breath tickles my ear.

"Can I help you?" Miss Opie's shadow falls over me.

Yes, you can help me reverse my wishes, and make everyone normal again.

"I'm doing a project for school. I need a picture of an elephant."

"She needs a picture of an elephant," Jamie echoes. He is excited about all this.

"What kind of picture?" She looks down at me.

"I need Ganesh!" I blurt out.

I have given myself away.

"Of course." Miss Opie doesn't bat a lash as she leads me to a section showing world religions and pulls out a book. My heart races.

I take the book, and Jamie and I sit at a table in the corner. I can't, *won't* look into his gray eyes.

I flip through the book and there it is—a photograph of Ganesh carved in stone. He has many arms and carries different objects, but it's his smiling face. This Ganesh is dancing, his arms up, one leg up, his big belly sticking out.

I check out the book, shove it in my knapsack and run home.

Jamie leans an arm against the door and gazes down at me with that handsome face to die for.

"Can I come in?" He looks crestfallen when I shake my head. "Don't wait outside," I say. "Go on home. I need my beauty rest." I promise to call him later, and finally he leaves. I'm not sure he has gone beyond our backyard.

Then I set the next stage of the backup plan in motion.

Red Rover, Red Rover, I call Psycho over, and she shows up a minute later in my parka and scarf, her face pale. "Maya, this is so cool. I feel like a secret agent. How did I do?"

"You did a fantastic job." I pat her on the back.

In my room, we open the book to the Ganesh page and place a lighted candle on either side of the book.

"Got the candy?" Psycho asks.

I take out the candy I bought before Ganesh disappeared.

We arrange everything around the book.

"Are you sure this will work?" she asks.

"It has to!" We shut off the light, so that only the candles illuminate the page, and sit cross-legged on the floor to play Ouija.

"Calling Ganesh," I say as we place our fingers on the message indicator. "Big-bellied Lord of the Enormous Ears. Lambodara—"

I wish I could remember all his names. I know this is not his favorite. I riffle through the pages for his other names, but only one is written there, Ganapati.

Psycho stares at the message indicator.

"Don't press so hard," I say crossly.

"I'm not."

The indicator doesn't move.

"Ganesh, we have S-W-E-E-T-S for you," I say.

Nothing.

"Maybe if you say we have Jelly Bellies?" Psycho asks.

Still nothing.

"Cherry Blossoms!" I say. "Mackintosh's Toffee. Ganesh, it's all here for the taking."

Candlelight flickers across the ceiling.

The message indicator begins to move, slowly at first, then faster. In a rush, the indicator spells DONKEY, CHANTER, NOSE and STUPID.

"Maybe Ganesh is an evil spirit, and we're doomed!" Psycho says.

"How can you even think that? He's a happy helper who grants boons. He can't control what people wish for." But Dr. Ghose's warning echoes in my mind. *Be careful. He's a bit of a trickster.*

Psycho shrugs. "Maybe he got confused, or maybe he isn't what he seems. Did you think of that?"

I frown. She could be right. There is no way I can understand everything about Ganesh. Maybe he only pretended to be a benevolent god.

No, his eyes were gentle.

"He warned me not to rush," I say. "He told me I would grow on my own, in time. So let's keep trying. He has to come back."

"Whatever you say, boss." Psycho's orange hair shines in the candle glow. She concentrates on the board, rests her fingers lightly on the message indicator.

I stare at her, and warmth wells up inside me.

"Thank you," I say.

"For what?" She looks up.

"For being my friend, for standing up to Brian Brower, for believing in Ganesh, even though you couldn't see him."

"Hey, what are friends for?" She grins, a glint of mischief in her eye.

We try and try to summon Ganesh, but there is no breath of air on my neck and no trace of his tinny voice. The book lies motionless on my desk, and finally the candle flames waver and die.

DOMINO RIPPLES

THE Ghoses are home. I fall over myself to go to their house for supper. I love Mrs. Ghose's cooking, I tell Mum. I love the smell of their house. I adore their charming sons. Dr. Ghose's stories about stomach problems are enthralling.

This time, Mrs. Ghose doesn't comment about my braces or how thin I am, and she doesn't notice Mum's blank eyes or Dad's nothing expression. The sweet chocolate scent of brownies replaces the reek of underarm sweat.

"Bhalo-Maya!" Mrs. Ghose pinches my cheeks.

I grab her soft shoulders. "Do you remember me from before? With braces and pimples? Skinny?"

She throws Mum a worried look. "Has Maya become feverish? She is making no sense."

Mum smiles.

I let go of Mrs. Ghose's shoulders. "You don't remember."

She pats my cheek. "I remember you when you were *choto*, this high."

"When did I change, Mrs. Ghose?"

"Call me Auntie! Auntie Mitil." She tilts her head sideways.

I try again. "When did I become pretty, Auntie? Wasn't I different the last time you saw me?"

Only now I realize I'm speaking in Bengali.

"Different? You are always lovely. Come."

She shoves me down the hall, away from my parents, and even the hallway has changed. The light shines more brightly and the walls are pink, not white.

As Mrs. Ghose throws me into the family room with the boys, who are playing an advanced version of Pong, a dark worry moves into me. Maybe my wishes are slowly changing the universe. How? Dad might call this the domino effect. My wishes are dominoes falling over and messing up reality.

I slip out of the room and up the stairs. I have the bedroom door halfway open when I hear someone panting behind me.

I slam the door and whip around.

Sahadev comes running down the hall, his hair parted on the wrong side, cowlick sticking out. He's at the age when he doesn't care what he looks like.

If only I were a kid again!

"Maya!" He smiles. "What are you doing?"

"Looking for the washroom. I forgot where it was." I'm so close to Ganesh, I can feel his smile.

"There's one downstairs."

"You told me to go upstairs last time."

"That's 'cause the toilet overflowed downstairs." He wanders away.

That was more than I needed to know.

I slip into the master bedroom. No telling what the Ghoses will do if they find me here. I have to do this alone, without Dr. Ghose peering over my shoulder.

The many-armed elephant gazes at me with wooden eyes. His face is long and thin, his grin tinged with malevolence.

I take a few Jelly Bellies from my pocket, arrange them around his feet and press the palms of my hands together in prayer.

"Please come back, Ganesh," I whisper. I explain what has happened and how I need him to set things right. I squeeze my eyes shut, open them. Nothing.

A sharp ache comes to me. I miss the golden Ganesh with the tinny voice and one ear flopping forward. What I would do to see that belly jiggle, to hear his crunching. To talk to him.

Either I dreamed him, or I have to factor him into what I know of the universe. Not that I understand how the universe works or how my Ganesh really got here, if he did.

Now he's gone.

I need someone to talk to, someone who knows.

Besides Ganesh, there is only one other person I can think of.

QUELLE IDÉE

I find Ms. Redburn in her office, reading *Wilderness Women*. She jumps when I get to her desk, and presses a hand to her chest above her WonderBra boobs.

"You startled me, Maya! Sit, sit."

I'm scaring people these days.

Today Ms. Redburn has on a soft yellow sweater. Her mole is a beauty mark enhancing her features. Why didn't I notice this before? She wouldn't be herself without that mole. Her mustache belongs on her face too. What I really notice are her eyes, green and deep, a forest <u>full of</u> sunlight.

I sit in the chair across from her desk, clasp my hands

in my lap. Words were crowding to come out, but now they stick in my throat.

She rests the book facedown on the desk. "Are you all right?"

"Yes. I mean no." I start to tell her about Ganesh and my wishes. I tell Ms. Redburn because I have to, because if I don't, I'll burst.

I keep talking even though she'll say I'm crazy and send me to the school nurse. She won't remember Mum's telling her we're moving. She won't remember the world before.

Still, I tell her about my too-perfect life, about my parents and Pinky and Jamie.

Ms. Redburn listens and nods, then opens her desk drawer and takes out a box of Jelly Bellies. "Have a few. They're my favorite."

She pops a handful into her mouth and chews. I take a Lemon one, and the sweet taste brings the world into focus. Sitting here with Ms. Redburn, eating candy and telling her about a talking golden elephant and zombie parents feels so natural.

She leans back in her chair and runs her fingers through her tangled hair. It's a pretty tangle now. I never noticed.

"I guess I'm doomed," I say finally. "I made my bed and now I have to lie in it."

"You say you tried to bring this . . . Ganesh back?"

"I tried everything. A picture, the Ghoses' statue, extra candy."

Ms. Redburn scrapes her chair back, gets up and comes around the desk with her arms outstretched.

"You need a hug," she says.

The tears come then, in great streaks down my cheeks. Finally, I pull away and Ms. Redburn sits on the corner of her desk, tipping it with her weight.

"Growing up isn't easy, is it?" she says.

Is that what I'm doing, growing up? "No, I guess it isn't."

"I was scared too, moving from Minnesota."

"You moved up from the States?"

She nods. "My mother died when I was eight. Dad was from Calgary, so he moved us back there. We moved a lot, from city to city. I came here because I wanted to settle in a small town for a while."

I try to imagine Ms. Redburn as a little girl. A round marshmallow girl with a mole, tangled black hair and a mustache. I wonder if kids made fun of her.

"What are you afraid of most?" she asks.

Good question. "I'm afraid that things will stay the way they are. That my parents and Jamie will turn into vapor. I'm afraid they'll stay trapped inside my wishes."

The glasses slip down her nose. "I'm glad you came to see me, Maya."

"But you can't help, can you? Please don't tell anyone what I said about Ganesh. They'll think I'm crazy."

Ms. Redburn pops a Very Cherry Jelly Belly into her mouth. "I won't tell anyone."

I get up and head for the door. Though I'm sure

nothing has changed, the weight has been lifted. Someone else knows.

"Maya, wait."

I turn, hoping for a miracle.

She gets up and paces, forefinger pressed to her chin. "Maybe you need to take radical action."

"Radical?"

"Sometimes you must do what's necessary to set things right. You have to find your own way, your own Ganesh. No other Ganesh will do."

"How can I find him?"

She pops more candy into her mouth. "You say your parents will say yes to anything. You may have to ask for a journey. Sit down. I have an idea."

CHAI, CHAI

I sit next to Dad on the Visva Bharati passenger train leaving Howrah Station. From here, express trains lead to nearly every major city in India. We're traveling north to the village of Santiniketan. The promise of Ganesh pulled me halfway around the world.

I keep a box of Jelly Bellies in my sweater pocket. Dad is reading the *Statesman*, holding the newspaper close to his face. My internal clock has turned upside down. I'm always thirsty. Grime coats my skin, settles in the crease of my chin, lights on my hair and eyelashes.

People walk close together, their bodies touching, and nobody cares. Men climb onto the roof of the train, their sinewy legs dangling off the side. The compartments, with no doors or curtains, swell to bursting with families. Excitement buzzes in the air. Christmas is coming, and with it the Paus Mela in Santiniketan, where Pinky has gone to our family's vacation home.

Home. What does it mean? Was my home on the prairie? In my town, with my real parents? My real parents live only inside me now. Zombie-Dad rides the train with me. Zombie-Mum has been left behind in Manitoba while my real Mum flits through the dark, searches for a way into the light.

Above our house, the northern sun will be rising over the Winnipeg River. A different sun, a white globe made of ice. Below, the fields spread and roll and unfold beneath spacious skies. The blue spruce, the crab apple trees and snow and flat Manitoba highways—all are ghost images whispering through me, here and then gone. I no longer know whether this other life existed at all.

There is only this day sitting hot and hazy in my brain. Sharp smells saturate me like dirty dishwater soaking into a sponge—the stench of sewage blending into cow dung, exhaust and sandalwood perfume. Elbows are used as often as horns. Street signs are just for show, and cows, chickens and dogs direct traffic; the cars are massive Ambassadors, with big, round headlights and broad fenders.

On the way to the train station, we passed curbside

barbers, children bathing at water pumps in the streets and hundreds of cycle rickshaws with barefoot drivers. We took the busy Howrah Bridge across the Hooghly River. I thought the platform would collapse beneath the weight of buses, taxis and pedestrians. Dad says this is coming home, but I don't belong here, though I was born in Calcutta. Born into possibility while so many others did not have choices.

Ganesh is everywhere, carved in stone over temple entrances, on doors, in clouds, in fingerprints smeared on the compartment window. At the edge of my vision he grins; then I realize it's dust in my eye.

None of these Ganeshes is my Ganesh.

I must find Pinky. Fast! But nothing moves quickly here. This train will leave sometime today; who knows when?

These seats are narrow and don't recline. A large, triple-chinned woman in a sari sitting across from me keeps staring. I look out the window, yawn and pretend to be sleepy. People here are even nosier than I am. They stare and stare and stare, as if I'm stark naked or I'm an alien from Pluto.

I try to watch anything and everything but the triple-chinned woman. I remember the long plane ride with my knees pressed against the seat in front of me, turbulence over London. A million shots just to get here: hepatitis, typhoid, cholera. I'm stiff with chemicals in my body. All this and I have no idea whether Pinky still has Ganesh.

I watch people out on the platform, rushing back and forth—women in saris or salwar kameezes, men in business suits, all striding past naked toddlers playing in the dirt. Skinny children in rags hold out their hands and call *"Ma, paisa."* Where are their parents?

These are India's lost children, more lost than I am. I want to help them, and help the kittens wandering along the tracks, the bony white cows, the stray mangy dogs. I could have helped them. But look what I used my wishes for.

Finally, the steam train hisses and groans away from the station. Scenery pours by in streams of brilliant color. We roll past green rice fields and miles of square mustard plots through which bony oxen pull makeshift wooden carts.

I picture children inside mud huts with thatched straw roofs. Reading by what lamp at night? A candle? Is it pitch-black inside, or do the stars and moon offer light? Could I have wished light for them?

A little boy calls "Chai, chai," and rattles on in nasal Bengali as he totters down the aisle, a tray of ceramic cups swaying in his hand. His tattered jeans and a button-down polyester shirt hang limp on his body. His face and hands are clean, his hair combed and slicked back. He wears a wrinkled shoulder bag, which probably contains all his possessions.

I focus on the click-click of the train along the tracks, growing faster and faster. I listen to the pieces of conversation, shouts in foreign languages. Some words are familiar, others not, and the odors of smoke and spice swirl through me.

Dad folds the newspaper just so. He never used to fold anything just so.

He gathers a few paisa from his pocket. Coins in another language, from another country.

When the little boy comes by again, Dad and the triple-chinned woman push money at him. The boy hands the woman a cup, which she extends to me.

"You are thirsty," she says in Bengali.

"Oh, no thanks—you drink it." I push the tea back toward her.

She clucks her tongue as two pigtailed girls race through the corridor, nearly knocking the chai boy off balance.

"She's only trying to be friendly," Dad whispers in my ear.

I smile and nod and tell the triple-chinned woman that my Dad is buying tea for me.

She gives the sideways nod and settles back, pulling her shawl around the choli, the top worn with a sari.

Maybe I've offended her. I understand Bengali, but Ganesh didn't help me understand the cultural details.

The boy has not given us our tea. He wheezes, leans against the doorjamb. Beads of sweat break out on his forehead.

"Are you all right?" I ask in Bengali.

"Hah, hah. Just one second." He balances the tray in one hand. "I'm fine."

"You're not, you're out of breath!"

He pants, and white patches appear around his nostrils.

"He's got heart trouble," the triple-chinned woman says in perfect English. I look at her.

The boy's face doesn't change, as if he doesn't understand.

"He's so young! How do you know?" I ask.

"He told me so. Every week I take the Visva to visit my daughter, and every week Darpan is here, peddling chai. Every week he is coughing and gasping."

His name, Darpan, means mirror.

"You're too young to work," I say. He must be Sahadev's age. I imagine the Ghose boys playing video games.

"Ne, Didi." Darpan laughs as if I have just said the moon is a balloon. He calls me sister.

"Why don't you see a doctor?"

He gives the sideways nod but doesn't answer.

"He hasn't the money. The operation is six thousand rupees." The woman shakes her head sadly.

"What about your parents? Can't they help?" I ask Darpan.

"His parents are in Madras," the woman says.

"Dad, where's Madras?"

"On the south coast, many miles away," Dad says.

"Where are we now, exactly?"

"West Bengal, on the western delta of the Ganges River. To the north lie the Himalayas." His voice comes out in a monotone, as if he's reading the answer from a book. My real dad would go on about Darjeeling and all his Very Oldest Friends.

"You're a long way from home!" I tell Darpan as he gives us our chai. He manages not to spill a drop as the train sways around a bend.

"You and I are not so different, then," he says, and I don't have a chance to ask what he means. He's already gone, singing "Chai, chai," down the aisle.

Dad gulps his tea, his eyes blank, but I am not so hasty. I hold the hot ceramic cup in my hand. Its shape is foreign, the liquid inside thick and frothy. I have a sudden understanding that chai is made with goat's milk, only I don't know how I know.

"Go on, drink," the triple-chinned woman says.

"Is it safe?"

She nods sideways. "One must take a few chances, nah? Otherwise life is not worth living."

THE HEART OF THINGS

WE arrive at a crowded train station with tile floors in vibrant color. We're in a world of red dust. As we step outside, a hundred rickshaw-wallahs crowd in, their voices a chorus inviting us to ride. Then a tall woman alights from a rickshaw and glides toward us in her silver sari. She stands a hundred feet tall with white tresses flowing like the mythic hair of Shiva. I know who she is right away.

Arms outstretched, she envelops Dad in a steel-grip hug, the bone-deep anguish of missing.

"Babi, Babi," she whispers. Her eyes glisten with tears.

I've heard only Pinky call Dad Babi. Babi-Mama.

I can't speak for the lump in my throat as Auntie hugs me with the same fervor, as if I've known her all my life.

"Ah, Maya, how you've grown." She cups my face in her hands. She smells familiar, of spice and silk, as if we have a secret family recipe of smells. The three of us jump into the bicycle rickshaw pedaled by a skinny man with sinewy black legs. His strength surprises me as he cuts through the crowd.

We cross gentle hills made of red soil, pass barefoot children, goats, chickens and young men and women with blond hair and tanned skin, riding rickety bicycles through the dirt.

"Who are they?" I ask.

"German visitors," Auntie says in Bengali. "They come for the open-air university. They seek sanctuary."

Sanctuary? I suppose I've come for the same reason, to seek refuge from my wishes. To seek forgiveness from Ganesh.

I'm squished between Dad and Auntie, who touches my wrist as she talks. I can't tell where my wished-for world ends and the real world begins. India is the inside-out, upside-down other side of me.

Auntie nods with the Indian head tilt, which is as normal here as red soil and goats wandering along the lanes. "Babi, I've made your favorite fish curry."

"Wonderful!" Dad says in Bengali.

I know what spices she uses in the curry, though again I don't know how I know. Fenugreek, cumin seed, *kalonji* and fennel.

"Where are we, Auntie?" I ask, to get my bearings.

"Westernmost corner of Bengal, nah?" She points out sal and palash trees, spindly and exotic, as well as jamun and mango groves. She says the name of this town means abode of peace. I am here, alive and aware. I have not disappeared inside myself since we got off the train.

We whiz past a group of wandering singers, their voices high-pitched and keening. I think of *The Bremen-town Musicians* with a pang, of Psycho's caterpillar eyebrow, Sally's turned-inward eye and the real Jamie's voice in my ear, *professor*.

"Has Pinky arrived?" I ask.

Auntie nods.

Relief! "I need to find her and Ganesh. The little golden statue."

"Ah yes. Ganesh, son of god Shiva and goddess Parvati."

Auntie adjusts her sari. "I know many stories about all the gods, but Ganesh is my favorite. His parents once gave their sons a difficult task. The first one to ride around the world would become the favorite son.

"Ganesh's brother was strong, confident in his ability. He stretched his muscles, mounted his peacock and sped away. Ganesh, with his rotund belly and sweet tooth, finished eating his mangoes."

I imagine my Ganesh shoveling Jelly Bellies into his golden mouth.

"Ganesh produced a pet mouse," Auntie goes on. "He stroked the mouse's fur, then sat on its back, and the mouse carried him a short distance before turning to circle the parents.

" 'My beloved parents,' Ganesh said. 'You are my whole world. I have traveled around my whole world.' His parents enfolded him in their arms, and he became their favorite son."

"So Ganesh played a trick on them," I say.

"A loving one," Dad pipes in, "but yes, a trick."

※ ※ ※

Auntie's vacation bungalow is at the end of a dusty red road. Pink and white roses bloom in abundance in the garden surrounded by a mud wall. My palms sweat as I scan the windows and the yard for Pinky. When I see her, what will I say? Will she flee? Grab Ganesh and run? Does she still have him?

My aunts, uncles and cousins of all shapes and sizes gather here from all over India. They spill from Auntie's house into the gardens. She introduces me, and the names weave through my mind, some staying, some lost. My cousin Joyantoni, round-faced and laughing, and my aunts Nina and Mira. These two aunts have green eyes, while Joyantoni's eyes are blue-rimmed, as if lit from the inside.

There's no sign of Pinky in the group sitting on benches around a roaring bonfire. The flames rush and crackle.

My family forms a sacred circle. Everyone holds hands and sways in unison as they sing Tagore songs in haunting harmony. I understand the words as if I always knew them: *I came out on the chariot of the first gleam of light, and pursued my voyage through the wildernesses of worlds leaving my track on many a star and planet. . . .*

The circle breaks to make room, and I slip onto the bench between two aunts. I see flickers of myself in their faces, hear my voice in their voices, see my hands in their gestures, only they reflect the old Maya, not the new. My relatives have not changed.

How I long for home, for my real self, braces and all. My Indian family showers me with love and acceptance, praises me for speaking Bengali. They ask about the flight, my studies, my health, my mum. Dad is off talking to my uncles, and happiness glows in his dark eyes. Even Zombie-Dad is at home in India. No matter which Dad he is, this is where he came from.

My mind wanders through stories and laughter. Great-aunt Rohini rode deer and battled crocodiles. Mira recently survived typhoid fever.

The worst illness I've ever had is chicken pox.

An uncle is in Darjeeling tending his tea gardens.

I think of our tin of First Flush tea leaves, sitting on the Formica countertop on the other side of the world. How distant my town seems, how mundane.

"Good you have come," Auntie says. "It's about time."

Little does she know. Time is running out. I begin to

wonder whether Pinky doesn't want to be found. What if she escaped to the Himalayas, the desert or the Bay of Bengal? She could be anywhere. I might spend the rest of my life searching. I'll be Wandering Chanticleer-Maya with my red rooster comb, forever looking for home.

Auntie rests a hand on my shoulder. "What is it, Maya? You are troubled."

"May I use the washroom?"

"Toilet? You needn't ask such a thing. Our home is your home."

"Thank you, Auntie." I break out of the circle and run into the bungalow, to find an open living area with a concrete floor. A group of men and women are discussing politics, problems in Kashmir, riots near Agra. The house smells of dust, incense and curried fish. A sizzling sound comes from a back room, probably the kitchen.

When my relatives see me, they exclaim, all in a jumble, "Maya! Come and sit." "Last time we saw you, you were just this small." "How she has grown." "You must tell all." "You look exactly like your mother." "We remember your mother from when she was this big." "Your parents were both so young. They were a love marriage. Did you know this? Not arranged."

My parents' marriage was not arranged, but I have arranged their lives.

I scan the room. Pinky isn't here.

"Where's the washroom?" I ask.

Everyone points toward a back hallway.

I rush by, my heart aflutter.

This washroom is nearly as big as my bedroom. The floor is made of concrete. There's a cracked porcelain sink and a toilet with a tank high on the wall, a chain dangling. I've never seen such a thing. I take a deep breath and try to think of a plan.

Then a knock comes on the door. Before I can answer, a dark girl in a faded red sari pokes her head in, and I know she's a servant. She keeps her gaze on the floor and hands me a roll of toilet paper as rough as sandpaper.

"Oh—thank you." I have already learned that Indians don't use toilet paper. They use water from a tap built into the wall next to the toilet.

The servant leaves, and I put the toilet paper on the sink and slip out into the hallway. I turn left, away from the living room.

I am in a bedroom. Thin mattress on a board, closet, mirror and nothing else. The room smells faintly of silk and mothballs. Despite the laughter and noise, the house feels simple and calm, an abode of peace.

No sign of Pinky or Ganesh.

I wend my way outside to the bonfire. Auntie puts an arm around me, and her eyes fill with affection.

"I need to find Pinky," I say.

Aunt Nina turns to me. "Did you say Pinky? She has gone to the Mela."

"The Mela! What about Ganesh? Her statue. Where is he?"

"Why, she has taken him with her, of course. To sell."

"To sell! But why?" This can't be. My insides turn cold.

"She is wanting a special brocade silk sari—"

"She's trading Ganesh for a sari?" I should have guessed. I jump to my feet. "I have to go."

Auntie touches my arm. "You may not find Pinky so easily. Thousands go to the Mela."

"I'll have to take my chances."

Otherwise, life is not worth living.

PAUS MELA

DAD and I take a rickshaw to the Paus Mela. A shroud
of dust covers the field, and the high-pitched strains of
mournful song drift over the crowd. All ages come to the
Mela—babies, toddlers, children, men and women from
young to very old. I think of the wheel of life, the past
and the future, the beginning and the end.

Local craftspeople sell their wares. Folk artists per-
form on makeshift stages. A boy jostles me, a girl whizzes
by and a chicken scuttles across my path. How will I find
Pinky in this craziness? And if I find her, how will I get
her to surrender Ganesh?

I scan the sea of heads. There, a flash of a sari, or there. No, it was only a girl who looks like Pinky.

Dad and I wander along the rows. Women sell saris woven with untwisted silk. How do I know this? Ganesh must have given me this information. If I find him and reverse the wishes, I may lose my new knowledge.

It doesn't matter. I can always learn again.

Night falls in a haze of neon lights. Still no Pinky. A sari trails around a corner, and I'm sure I see her. We rush past children buying wooden toys and mothers choosing palm-leaf trinkets, merchants sitting cross-legged in lotus position on the ground, piles of silver jewelry—rings, bangles, anklets and nose rings—laid out before them. In every girl or woman, I see Pinky's face.

Then I spot her running ahead. She disappears in the crowd. Women jostle me. Children tug at my jeans, begging for money. Elbows poke at my ribs. Shouts, and the smells of burning dung, frying pakoras, curry.

I whirl around, trying to see Pinky. Dad stays close. He doesn't ask why I'm running. Why I bump into people. There's the flash of a black braid, the glint of gold, Pinky's mocking smile.

I run down one path, then another. Hands reach out, clawing, demanding I pay for silver bangles, ankle bells, earrings. Statues of goddesses and gods glare from grotesquely painted faces, bodies poised in dance or the act of killing demons. None of them is Ganesh. Then I turn a corner and see piles of glittering brocade saris, and the back of Pinky disappearing around the bend.

Oh, Ganesh. Are you teasing me? Is this one of your tricks?

Then I see Pinky again, rushing away.

I dash after her, leaving Dad behind, and grab the edge of her shawl.

"Where have you been? Where's Ganesh?" I gasp.

"Let go of me." She wrestles from my grip, spins around to glare. My heart sinks when I see the glittering green brocade sari folded beneath her arm.

"No, no! You can't have traded Ganesh!" I gasp for breath.

"I should not have." Her voice is ice. "The statue was worth ten times this sari."

"Then why did you?"

A storm cloud of yearning darkens her eyes. "I have wanted this sari ever since I can remember. I want to be beautiful."

I step back and bump into Dad. "What is it, Maya-baby? I nearly lost you!"

Pinky and I lock glares. She knows I need Ganesh. She cannot know why.

"You have no idea what you just did," I shout. "This is worse than you know!"

"I hope you and Jamie live happily ever after together." Pinky's acid voice sears me as she turns on her heel.

I'm stunned. Then I race back to the sari merchant, a wrinkled woman with white hair and a jewel-studded nose ring.

"A girl just traded Ganesh—I need him." I must look crazy, sweating, with my hair flying wild.

The woman shakes her head. "Nah, nah. Ganesh-nah."

"You're lying!"

Dad comes up behind me. "What is she lying about?"

"She has Ganesh! Help me."

Dad rattles off a string of sharp sentences I can't comprehend.

The woman replies in the same sharp tongue, waves her arms and shakes her head.

Dad turns to me. "Her husband is selling Ganesh. Come."

He weaves through the crowd. I follow, and there, before me, are hundreds of statues of Hindu gods and goddesses—Shiva, Vishnu, Lakshmi, Durga, Kali, Sarasvati—displayed on a blanket on the ground. There are rows and rows of Ganeshes in wood, gold, silver, brass; sitting, standing, and dancing.

Which Ganesh is my Ganesh?

MAYA RUNNING

"YOU want Durga? Parvati?" The merchant pushes a statue at me. "Only two hundred rupees! Brahma? Indra, Agni, the god of fire?"

I shake my head, scan the Ganeshes. Sitting, dancing, reclining; five-headed, many-armed.

"Which one is yours?" Dad asks.

"I don't know, I don't know!"

The merchant points to a brass statue of Kali, a frightening four-armed goddess with her tongue sticking out. She wears a garland of human skulls. In one hand she holds a sword, in the other a severed demon's head.

"Ah, you like!" The merchant grabs the statue.

Oh no. He won't stop. "No, I want Ganesh. Ganesh!"

"Kali kills demons!" the merchant says. "You know Kali? Kali-cutta?"

"Yes, yes!" I squint at the back row of Ganeshes, partly hidden behind taller statues of Shiva and Vishnu.

"She was so angry that the earth shook and mortals feared for their lives."

"Ganesh!" I plead, searching the back row. *There.* I recognize the curve of the gold. My Ganesh is the only statue with one floppy ear.

"That one!" I scream.

The merchant scoops up a red statue.

"No, the one beside it, to the left!"

He lifts my Ganesh, and I can hardly contain myself.

"Very valuable, nah? Six thousand rupees!" the merchant yells.

"I don't have six hundred dollars. Dad!"

Dad fumbles in his pockets.

The merchant gets a greedy look.

I snatch Ganesh. I am turning, running away.

I have never stolen in my life.

Correction. I have stolen from my parents' night-stands. I'm running, running as fast as I can, and I hear shouting behind me. I glance back to see a fire blazing at a curry stand. A crowd gathers, throwing water on the flames. No sign of my pursuers, but they're coming.

I can run fast, and now I run on air.

I smuggle Ganesh out of the Mela, hiding him in my sweater pocket with the Jelly Bellies.

Perhaps Dad is looking for me. For now, he will have to look. The world is about to change. I am sweating from running. I hope Ganesh can still hear my apologetic thoughts, hope he's not nauseated from bouncing around in my pocket.

When I get far away, I kneel in the red dust beneath a banyan tree. I catch my breath, pull Ganesh from my pocket.

He's heavy and cool in my hands.

I clear dirt away from the gnarled roots and place him on a flat spot. Hardly daring to breathe, I arrange the Jelly Bellies around him.

Please talk, I'm thinking, because I know you can read my mind.

I sit cross-legged facing him, close my eyes and concentrate. "Ganesh, I miss you. Lord of the Enormous Ears, Great One . . ."

It is disconcerting to stare at the elephant face stuck in an unchanging, generous smile. None of Ganesh's living warmth glows within.

"You love Jelly Bellies," I say.

Nothing.

"Please restore my family," I say to the golden face. "And the world. My wishes were a river with an undertow." My voice cracks. I twist my hands together in my lap. Behind the banyan tree, a red dust devil swirls up into the sky.

Still no movement from Ganesh.

I forge on, remembering how long it took to get from no to yes with Mum and Dad, back in the real world. I'll sit here until Ganesh gets from no to yes.

"Mum isn't herself," I say. "She wanted to leave our town, but I made us stay. Give her a life of her own."

Even as I say so, I remember how difficult life was before the wishes. Mum was slipping away to her future, to the university, to her own private California.

There's a pain in knowing this truth, but which life do I choose? Only an occasional flash of butterfly wings in the dark wood, or the real mother who is sometimes there, sometimes gone?

My voice wavers on a thread. "Give her back her true self. Dad too. And Jamie . . ."

I'm talking to myself, to the breeze, to the kaleidoscope of color in the coolness. I speak to the past, the future, the wheel of life. This is the only Ganesh who will ever listen, who can listen. But he's not here.

"My family must move," I say, my voice growing stronger. "That was what we were meant to do. I have to leave that town. I know that now. I should never have forced us to stay by wishing. Maybe I'll go back there someday, but for now . . . for now, Ganesh, I'm tired, so tired of being my own real parents."

I realize suddenly that this is what I've been doing.

Although I was lonely before, in my real life, when Mum and Dad were their true selves, distant from me, not really knowing me, they were still my parents.

Now I'm an orphan.

I talk and talk to Ganesh until my throat swells with dryness and dust coats my eyelids. Until I shiver with the cool of night, until a car rumbles up behind me. The engine kicks off, and a door creaks open and closed.

I grab Ganesh and tuck him into my pocket. As I gather up the Jelly Bellies, heavy footsteps approach behind me.

"Miss, are you all right?" a man asks.

I still understand Bengali.

There is nothing more to be done.

I don't want to turn and show my tearstained cheeks, but I have to.

He is a thin man in an olive green uniform. Maybe he thinks my tears are from religious ecstasy as I pray to the Remover of Obstacles.

"Come, come." He gently takes me by the elbow.

I stand up, feeling the weight of gold in my sweater pocket. There is no richness here for me.

The man drives me home in his Ambassador. My relatives gather at the gate. They are my family letting me know they care. Zombie-Dad smiles, doesn't scold me for stealing. He hasn't told anyone that *I* was the thief.

As I follow him into the bungalow, a deep sadness washes through me, but it's like when the snow first melts on the prairie and the grass is still brown, flattened underneath. I have to remember that the flowers will grow.

MAYA AND PINKY

PINKY turns in front of the mirror in the sparse bedroom and studies the image of herself wrapped in a billowing green brocade sari. When she glimpses me standing in the doorway, she frowns. I'm holding the lifeless statue of Ganesh behind my back.

"I look ridiculous," she says, hands on her hips.

"You look beautiful," I say, although to my surprise, the green silk overpowers her delicate features. Funny, her beauty shone through better when she wore my faded Levi's.

She sighs. "For so long I thought I wanted this pattern, the brocade. Now I am not certain. . . ."

"Sometimes what you think you want isn't what you really want at all."

She sits on the bed, the sari deflating around her. "Hah, you speak the truth. I shall have to return the sari. Of course I can't walk around looking like an unripe jackfruit."

I sit beside her and put Ganesh in her lap. Her eyes light up for a moment, then her brows knit together. "Look at his floppy ear. This is my Ganesh! You bought him back?"

"Actually, I stole him."

"You what? Why would you steal him?"

I can't tell her about my wishes. She wouldn't believe me.

"For you. Sorry, Pinky. I'm sorry I was jealous of you. I thought you were stealing my friends, and all along, you were just being yourself."

She looks at me, then hands Ganesh back. "No need to explain. You keep Ganesh. You've become attached to him. Now he is yours."

"How can you give him to me after all I've done to you?"

"What have you done to me?"

If only she knew the whole story. "I was jealous of your dancing, of your Indianness. I didn't realize that I have a touch of India inside me too. I ruined your trip to Canada."

"The trip was not a complete loss, but I am glad to be home."

"I've told lies about a lot of things. How can you forgive me?"

"I don't see what there is to forgive." She touches my cheek. Her fingers are soft.

I bite my lip. "Are you sure?"

She nods. "Perhaps I'll pick up Ganesh on my next visit to Canada. Place him inside your front door, touch his feet when you step into the house, and he shall bring you good fortune."

Good fortune. The words, once blazing with promise, smolder and crumble.

"I can't keep him," I say. "He doesn't belong to me. He doesn't belong to anyone." Ganesh is off circling the world, churning the oceans, playing tricks on the gods.

"You found him again at the Mela, so you were meant to keep him."

No, you don't understand, I want to tell her. *I called and called, but he never returned.*

"I'm sorry about your nose," I say, although the scar has faded to a fine line.

"Hah, it is nothing. I can tell my friends I have gone Krazy Karpeting."

We sit side by side, listening to laughter and conversation outside, the crackling of the bonfire.

The unspoken word *Jamie* hovers between us.

"Listen, I'd like you to have my jeans," I say.

"You mustn't give up your precious clothes for me."

"They make you look totally American."

"You mean Canadian." She laughs, then lowers her voice to a whisper. "I've met someone, a boy from a good family. Ma and Baba don't know yet, but they will love him."

"Where did you meet him?" I whisper.

"On the train from Cal. Coincidence, nah? He is soooo handsome. You mustn't tell anyone. No one must know I actually spoke to him, carried on and such. They will ask why have I ruined my reputation. And you mustn't tell them I've done such wild things, Krazy Karpeting with boys."

And kissing Jamie, I'm thinking.

"I won't tell, promise."

The starlight glimmers in Pinky's eyes. I take her warm hand, and relief floods through me. We're cousins again. My wishes weren't strong enough to suppress her nature after all.

THEY ALWAYS SAY

THE next afternoon, a rickshaw takes Dad and me back to the train station. The driver's feet point forward. Phew. He is not a demon.

I keep Ganesh in the knapsack in my lap. Or what was once Ganesh. I think of what he told me: *The session is now closed.*

Pinky returned the sari. I can still see her waving good-bye from the bungalow porch. She gave me a red stick-on bindi, which I wear on my forehead, for now. I said I would never do this, but things can change.

Of all my relatives, Pinky remains foremost in my thoughts. Odd. When you have done something bad to someone, you can't get him or her out of your mind.

Auntie begged me to stay, to get to know my family. How could I explain? Mum and Dad need me. I have to take care of them now.

A terrible weariness sweeps over me.

I lean against the window, close my eyes and give myself over to the hypnotic click of the train along the tracks, to Dad's voice asking if I need water, a pillow, if I am okay.

I say yes and listen to the strains of English, Hindi and Bengali mingling in the corridor. I think of children sitting in the dirt, their bellies filled with parasites but no food. They have no dad to take them home. They sit in the dirt until they die or someone rescues them.

Sometimes stubbornness and bravery can only take you so far. I have to make the best of this stuck world.

Dad leans back and begins to snore with his mouth open. Lucky, we have this tiny compartment to ourselves. A miracle.

Then, just as I'm drifting off, the knapsack moves in my lap. I nearly jump.

"Ganesh!" I shout, then cover my mouth.

Dad keeps snoring.

"Have you got more of the Licorice?" comes a muffled voice.

I unzip the knapsack. Ganesh's trunk swishes out. "Awfully hot in here. I am feeling motion sickness."

"I thought you were gone! You tricked me!" Tears sting my eyes. I shove a few candies into the bag.

"Ah, my favorite!" He munches away.

I wipe the tears from my cheek. "Why did you leave? You were gone!"

"Remember, you did not wish for me to stay."

"I needed you! My wishes messed up the world."

"Yes, child. I heard your shrill adolescent screeching from a distance."

"Why didn't you reply?"

Ganesh sighs. "I had pressing business in Darjeeling, and then I was delayed in Srinagar. I am here now, but this is the last time I shall appear in this statue. I must leave shortly. Hurry."

"Don't go. You have to help!"

Ganesh pokes his golden head out of my knapsack. "Help with what?"

"Did you hear what I said beneath the banyan tree?"

Dad snores in a rhythmic honk and whoosh.

"Let me try to remember. You may have to say again." Ganesh chomps another candy.

"Say all that again?"

I hear the sweet, melodic voice of Darpan calling "Chai, chai." Today he sounds like an angel, his voice a hymn drifting down from the heavens. As he draws near, he starts to cough.

"You have to reverse the wishes!" I whisper to Ganesh.

"Remember." Ganesh pauses to smack his lips. "I only removed obstacles. I can move things out of the way, but only you have the power to see the truth."

"I don't understand, Ganesh. Make the world the way it was. Return my real parents. They're gone."

Ganesh's eyes glint. His trunk points out the window. "That field, that tree, that cow. They are gone, but they were there, and they are still there. We have only passed them."

"What do you mean?"

"The answer lies within."

"You're not making any sense."

"What is it that your parents always say now?"

"Is this a riddle? Wait, someone's coming." I zip up the knapsack just as Darpan reaches our compartment. Not that he would be able to hear Ganesh speak, but I can't take the chance.

Darpan's eyes light up with happiness. "Free chai, free chai." He leans in the doorway, his chest heaving.

Dad lets out a loud snore, and Darpan chuckles. The same worn, tattered shirt hangs from his lean frame, and he wears the same wrinkled shoulder bag. He balances the tray of teacups without spilling. His face is pale, cheeks hollow. He wheezes, unable to catch his breath.

"No free chai! You sell the chai and keep the money."

I rummage in my pocket and hand him all I have left. Twenty rupees. Only about two dollars.

Darpan shakes his head, hands the money to me, but I don't take it. We go back and forth. Tea sloshes onto the tray, splashes onto Darpan's bare feet.

He won't last long with heart trouble and nobody to care for him. I can't leave him like this.

As if in a trance, I watch myself unzip the knapsack and remove Ganesh.

The gold flashes and Darpan's eyes widen in wonder.

In slow motion, Ganesh rolls out of my hand and into Darpan's shoulder bag.

"Sell the statue," I say to Darpan. My voice rasps, barely above a whisper. "He's made of solid gold. His eyes are diamonds. Sell him and go to the doctor."

"Ne, Didi!" Darpan tries to shrug off his bag, but I slide the strap back up on his shoulder.

"Go to school, send money to your family, do what you want, but get your heart operation. Promise, Darpan!"

"Promise."

Dad stops snoring but doesn't open his eyes.

"You are crying, *Didi*!" Darpan says.

I wipe the tears away.

Darpan's shoulder bag doesn't move, and I don't hear crunching. Oh, Ganesh! I am thinking. He doesn't reply. I can't feel him anymore. He is gone.

Dad starts to wake up. He yawns, stretches and blinks.

I feel the train rushing, smell the mustard fields, the air thick and rich, sunlight spilling in through the windows. It all slows as I think of what Ganesh told me. *What is it that your parents always say now?*

The answer has been staring at me all along.

ON MY OWN

DAD and I sleep through most of the flight from London to Canada. In Winnipeg, Mum picks us up at the airport. She is barely there, a thinly sliced parent on the burnt toast of life. I search in vain for a trace of my real Mum.

She hops into the passenger seat and lets Dad drive.

I get into the back, and as Dad turns on the motor, I lean over the seat.

"Mum, Dad. I have something to tell you. I want you to listen."

"Whatever you want, Maya," they answer in unison.

I take a deep breath, wishing Ganesh was here to hold my hand, to let me know everything will be okay. For now, I'm on my own. I think of Darpan, who will go to school and have his operation.

"Okay. This is what I want," I say clearly. "I want you to return to your normal selves. The way you were before I made my wishes. I am setting you free."

I hold my breath, and the earth groans to a stop on its axis. The snowflakes flutter down in surprise, and then Mum slowly turns.

"Well," she says, and a light snaps on in her eyes. "What do you think you were doing, gallivanting across the Atlantic without permission? Don't you know the rules?"

I grin at her. "Yes, I know the rules!"

Dad switches on the radio and whistles off-key to "I Can See Clearly Now." His Einstein eyes shine and I know his mind is racing out into the universe.

MAYASRI

THE early-morning sun sends brilliant rays across my sleeping bag. My bed is gone. The movers took everything except our camping gear and a few dishes. I slept on a lopsided air mattress in my empty, echoing room. My skinny body and braces are back, but I don't mind.

Two weeks ago, an airmail came from Pinky, along with a new photograph. She's even more beautiful than before. She writes less often now that she has a boyfriend. Her life is no longer boring.

I have been sitting here reading my autograph book. Everyone is into rhyming these days.

Dear Maya . . .
Throughout these years
I've been your friend,
So remember me till the very end,
And when you're old please don't forget,
Wherever you are I remember you yet.
Sally Weston

If Jamie Klassen lived across the sea,
What a good swimmer Maya would be.
Your friend,
Kathy Linton

May your life be like a grand piano,
Strong, upright and tall.
Never B flat
Sometimes B sharp
Always B natural
Sincerely,
Miss L. Barth

Down the road there is a tree,
On it says "Remember me."
Farther on there is a spot,
There it says "Forget me not."
Ms. Redburn

The circle is round
And has no end,

And that's how long
I'll be your friend
Psycho McCann

I think of Psycho, her orange hair fiery in the sun, and Sally, destined to wear lace-doily dresses to special events, and Ms. Redburn reading *Ms.* magazine. Their faces are so clear in my mind.

I tuck the autograph book into my travel knapsack, where my diary hides among Enid Blyton books and a sweater.

Mum pops her head in. "Dad and I are going shopping and to the post office. We'll be back in no time flat."

I roll up the sleeping bag and get dressed. Then I go to the kitchen and make tea with the one pot that hasn't been packed, sugar packets and powdered milk.

I walk through our house. A new family will move in and arrange new furniture, new curtains. Will they see ghosts of us? A shadow of Dad stoking the fire? Mum studying at the dining table? Me writing in my diary on my ghost bed?

I say good-bye to my bedroom, to the holes in the wall where I tacked my posters through the years. Good-bye to the washroom, the linoleum floor in patterns of green. I say good-bye to the family room, more linoleum. In the kitchen, I say good-bye to the refrigerator and stove.

Then good-bye to the basement, where we whacked tennis balls against the concrete wall, where the washing machine tilted off balance, then banged across the floor like a great monster. I go back upstairs and say good-bye to my parents' bedroom, which looks the least like part of our home now. No more nightstands or dressing table or bed, but the smell of Joy lingers in the air.

Outside, the sky stands a brilliant blue above melting snow. The air is warm and thick. My shoes slip in slush on the sidewalk. Robins send a chorus of spring tunes out into the breeze. It is possible that I'll never hear the birds sing here again.

We no longer have a bright mailbox at the end of our driveway, though I can still picture it in my mind. Nobody else seems to remember my dreamworld. I wonder what happened to the mailman. Maybe he's off delivering mail in someone else's wishes.

I wait in the yard, with my travel knapsack over my shoulder. It's Sunday. The town is quiet. Most of my friends are in church. It is spring in Manitoba, the maple leaves wet and matted. Spray-painted in a mist of green seeds, Siberian elm trees sway in the breeze. Fern sprigs rise, curled aliens at the base of tamarack trees.

I etch the light into my mind, the sun reflecting off the Winnipeg River. Bulrushes push up through the shallows. I let these memories of home soak in.

Home is the place that etches itself into you, that becomes part of you. I think of Darpan in India, his home. For me, India is a twilight country, dust in my eye, a place I had to go, where I will go again, but not today.

Today I'm leaving, and Jamie is sauntering around the corner. He carries a flat paper bag in one hand. Same open bomber jacket, combat boots, muscle shirt and jeans. There is a certain comfort in knowing what Jamie wears. In summer, he will take off the bomber jacket and wear the muscle shirt and jeans.

As he draws nearer, I try to memorize the shape of his face, so that later, when I close my eyes, I'll be able to see him.

He walks up our driveway and our gazes collide, bam. The mesmerized in-love eyes are gone. Jamie's gray eyes are back with his smile to die for.

He takes my hand. I'll always remember the warmth and pressure of his fingers holding mine.

"Did you hear what happened to Brian Brower?" he says.

I shake my head.

"He called Vishnu Ghose a nigger at the skating rink, and the two Ghose boys pushed him. He tripped and fell on the ice and broke two teeth. Then Mrs. Ghose yelled at him. Everybody heard."

"Oh!" I suppose I should feel victorious. Instead, I feel sorry for Brian Brower. He never got to have samosas for lunch. He didn't get to fly to India and see his relatives. He didn't get to learn another language. He doesn't have a mother like Mrs. Ghose to make papadums and pakoras and defend him when kids make fun of him.

I'll miss the Ghoses. I may never see them again. "I'll write from California. Promise you'll write too."

"Promise." Jamie lets go of my hand as the Chevy prowls around the corner and up the driveway. We step back onto the sidewalk, out of the way as my parents get out. Dad hands me a big envelope.

My full name and address are printed in neat blue ink. There is no return address, only an Ottawa stamp dated two days ago. The envelope is stiff and heavy. What could be inside? Pinky would've sent an airmail.

Mum, Dad and Jamie gather around as I tear open the seal. I pull out the latest issue of *The Maple Leaf Chronicles*. The magazine smells new.

Spring splashes across the glossy cover in tiger-lily orange and daffodil yellow. A slip of blue paper flutters out onto the ground. I pick it up and stare at my name in pretty handwriting along the line *Pay to the order of.*

Real money.

"Maya has a check." Dad does not sound surprised.

"Wow! Groovy." Jamie nods.

"Congratulations!" Mum hugs me.

There's another piece of paper tucked inside the magazine's front cover.

Dear Dr. and Mrs. Mukherjee,

Thank you for sending your daughter's story, "If You Could Only See It My Way." We share your belief that our readers will enjoy this tale told from the viewpoint of a blade of grass. We wish Mayasri the best of luck in her future endeavors.

Sincerely,
The Editors

❋ ❋ ❋

I fold the letter and hardly dare to breathe as I open the magazine. There it is, on page fifteen. "If You Could Only See It My Way."

I run my finger across the smooth page. My name does not smudge. It is spelled correctly, the ink permanently printed on paper.

"Maya, how wonderful! We're proud of you." Mum plants a kiss on my cheek.

Warmth comes into me. I smile at her, then at Dad. He opens the Chevy trunk and acts all busy transferring groceries to the cooler and arranging our camping gear. Jamie and Mum rush over to help, while I stand on the sidewalk, staring at my story.

Then, just like that, Ganesh's elephant-gold face superimposes itself on the page, clear as day, and winks at me.

Thought I'd left, did you? he says in my head.

You tricked me, I tell him in my mind, watching his trunk swish on the page. I suppose Ganesh appears where he wants to appear. I traveled around the world only to find him here, in a magazine.

I did not trick you, I only told you the truth. I remove illusions. Remember?

I nod, and Ganesh's face fades.

We pile into the car. I'm squished between our bags in the backseat. I roll down the window, and Jamie hands me the flat paper bag.

I open it and pull out a record album: Yes, *Fragile*.

208

"Thanks." I blink back tears.

Jamie stands aside, sadness in his eyes. The same sorrow sweeps through me.

"Bye," I whisper.

"Bye, professor. See ya 'round."

Dad revs the engine, backs the Chevy down the driveway and steers toward Massey Road.

I peer through the rear window and wave. Jamie waves back, and I watch him disappear around the bend.

I face forward again, take a deep breath.

Dad is picking his nose while driving, an eccentric habit of geniuses. In the passenger seat Mum gathers herself, her shoulders relaxed. She is decked out in jeans and a sweater for the road.

I sit up straight and watch the town rush by.

I am beginning to know who I am.

I am the only kid in this town who had a story published in *The Maple Leaf Chronicles,* the only kid who gets letters from Indian relatives connected to her by threads that can never be broken. I am changeable, as transient as the seasons. My mother and father, my ancestors, the dust and heat of India, the northern lights and the snow melting on the prairies—I am all of this and none of this. I am special in a way that is bigger and older than this town.

I am Mayasri Mukherjee.

ABOUT THE AUTHOR

ANJALI BANERJEE was born in India, grew up in Canada and California and received degrees from the University of California, Berkeley. At the age of seven, she wrote her first story, about an abandoned puppy she found on a beach in Bengal. Her Pushcart Prize–nominated fiction has appeared in several literary journals and in the anthology *New to North America*. She lives in the Pacific Northwest with her husband, three crazy cats and a black rabbit named Friday. Learn more about Anjali on her Web site: www.anjalibanerjee.com.